what's the story?

WEST YORKSHIRE VOL II

Edited by Donna Samworth

First published in Great Britain in 2004 by
YOUNG WRITERS
Remus House,
Coltsfoot Drive,
Peterborough, PE2 9JX
Telephone (01733) 890066

All Rights Reserved

Copyright Contributors 2003

SB ISBN 1 84460 310 5

FOREWORD

This year, Young Writers proudly presents a showcase of the best short stories and creative writing from today's up-and-coming writers.

We set the challenge of writing for one of our four themes - 'General Short Stories', 'Ghost Stories', 'Tales With A Twist' and 'A Day In The Life Of . . .'. The effort and imagination expressed by each individual writer was more than impressive and made selecting entries an enjoyable, yet demanding, task.

What's The Story? West Yorkshire Vol II is a collection that we feel you are sure to enjoy - featuring the very best young authors of the future. Their hard work and enthusiasm clearly shines within these pages, highlighting the achievement each story represents.

We hope you are as pleased with the final selection as we are and that you will continue to enjoy this special collection for many years to come.

CONTENTS

Renu Kumar   1

Bardsey Primary School
Charlotte Morgan	2
Heléna Kilroy	3
Oliver Frankel	4
Jamie Hammond	5
Olivia Dalrymple	6
Rhian Miles	7
Lauren Blackburn	8
Oliver Eastman	9
Christopher Ham	10
Hannah Sheerin	11
Megan Marshall	12
Hannah Donaghy	14
Rachel Bonney	15
Deborah Todd	16
Stephanie Douglas	18
Lucy Beddard	19
Jessica Procter	20
Lucy Nunn	21
Elysa Manning	22
Lisa Galinsky	23
Jennifer Smith	24
Amy Robertson	25
Rebecca Holder	26

Boothroyd J&I School
Ifsa Hussain	27
Harun Nawaz	28
Hannah Wilson	30
Akeel Javid	32

Fairburn CP School
Jodi Hartley	34
Thomas William Hetherington	35

Hayley Rhodes	36
Laura Coldwell	37
Georgina Barker	38
Stephen Lunn	39
Hannah Langley	40

Farsley Farfield Primary School

Yasmine Crawford	41
Alex Dimotsis	42
Danielle Hutchison	44
Alex Hawkhead	45
Adam Choudry	46
Mark Hodgson	47
Laura McNamara	48
Abigail Ramsden	49
Riswan Asghar	50
Emma Williamson	52
Melissa Porter	53
Jessica Sims-Walton	54
Emily Webster	55
Lauren Guest	56
William Buck	57
Rebecca Brown	58
Rachel Smith	59
Lucy Cross	60
Charlotte Wakefield	61
Joe Howard	62
Bethany Sommerville	63
Amy Slater	64
Jordan Cummings	65
Hollie Kent	66
Megan Ingram	67
Corri Stevenson	68
Holly Smith	69
Liam Hemingway	70
Nathanael Brown	71
Alexandra Fawcett	72
David Burrell	73

Lauren Hanson	74
Ashley Nicholson	75
Charlotte Beattie	76
Jessica Louise Nunn	77
Jacob Bowers	78
Samantha Stringer	79
Timothy Corcoran	80
Roberta Hall	81
Rebecca Laurie	82
Chloe Waite	83
Michaela Nutter	84
Jessica Townsley	85
Benjamin Matthews	86
Adam Wild	87
Connor Robinson	88
Lucy Maude	90
Amy Stevenson	91
Amy Mitchell	92
Jasmine Cheema	93
Jessica Williamson	94
Emily Killoran	95
Jordan Anderson	96
Jack Henderson	97
Cordell Sutton	98
Jennifer Burrell	99
Fay Walker	100
Michael Mullin	101
Dale Tunnicliffe	102
Bilal Salim	103
Patrick Miller	104
Victoria James	105
Alaina Benn	106
Abigail Morgan	107
Matthew Atter	108
Joe Sutcliffe	109
Emma Shaw	110
Jordan Halton	111
Daniel Anderson	112

Field Lane Primary School

Danielle Ramsden	113
Eve Hamill Murin	114
Benjamin Margison	115
Eve Morley	116
Victoria Noble	117
Stacey Thornton	118
Michelle Holland	119
Kayleigh McFarland	120
Melissa Jayne Hrab	121
Ben Shryane	122

Harewood CE Primary School

Dominic Siekierkowski	123
Thomas Crocker-Pleasant	124
Tesfya Gorebooth	125
Lorna Hulse	126
Imran Ali	127
Richard Moore	128
Sanjeet Choda	129
James Hartley	130
Manpreet Ryatt	131
Uzair Khan	132
Olivia Feldman	133
Jordan Appleson	134
Sophie White	135
Jamie Newall	136
Polly-Anna Bury	137
Elliot Williams	138
Jessica Walker	139
Hasan Malik	140
Simon Moore	141
Leah Feldman	142
Michael Gregson	143

Leeds Grammar School

William Lord	144
Robert Hooley	145

Sam Grant	146
Matthew McGoldrick	147
Dominic Wrench	148
Jonathan Letts	150
Robert Morgan	152
Richard Limb	153
Marco Sarussi	154
Michael Ballmann	155
Alistair Finerty	156
Edward Dean	157
Alex Walden	158

St Nicholas RC Primary School, Leeds

Gemma Boyle	159
Joseph Geddes	160
Sophie McBride	161
Sophie Staniforth	162
Bethany Parkin	163
Emma Ruiz	164
James Geddes	165
Philip Diamond	166
Rachel Cichorz	167
Louina Victor	168
Rebecca Baldwin	170
Kyle Hulme	171

Salterhebble JI School

Rebecca Walton	172
Chelsea Gledhill	173
Harriet Coleman	174
Melka Osman El-Amin	175
Adil Naeem	176
Zulaykha Afzal	177
Robert Alderson	178
Emily Grace Walker	179
Louise Greenwood	180
Darren Chapman	181
Sophia Nawaz	182

Josh Cocker	183
Kirsty Victoria Wells	184
Gemma Smith	185
Kayleigh Parkinson	186
Alex Anderson	187
Rebecca Fleming	188
Andrew McGuire	189
Emily Stansfield	190
Aakash Rana	191
Francesca Hardman Saião	192
Hannah Oxley	193
Maleeha Ahmad	194

Withinfields Primary School

Brandon Croft	195
Rhian Rothery	196
Deryn Kitson	197
Megan Bakes	198
Chloe Marsden	200
Ben Ward	201
Matthew Emmett	202
Ben Holdsworth	203
William Binns	204
Louise Doodson	205
Danny Quirk	206
Thomas Mawdsley	207
Matthew Triller	208
Chérie Patterson	209
Grace Metcalfe	210
Jake Lamb	211
Nicole Hodgson	212
Amy Clarkson	213
Ben Wickings	214
William Forsyth	215
James Eastwood	216
Rebecca Holden	217
Louisa King	218
Gemma McGall	219

The Stories

A Day In The Life Of Brutus - The Four-Legged Feline

I creep closer, swishing my tail, coming down wind so my prey can't smell me. The bird turns, twitters and takes to the sky with a cry, 'Can't catch me, you striped, four-legged monster!'
Then the human descended on me, saying, 'Would oo like a strokey-wokey? Would oo like a patty-watty?' (This gobbledegook is very strange. I can understand the Queen's English, you know!) They feed me though, so I can't complain, but the muck they feed me is unbelievable. Why don't they feed me plain meat? I'd much rather eat that than this dry kibble. And water? What happened to full cream milk? They let me sit by the fire, warming myself. I imagine I'm in some warm country, rather than damp old Britain. So rowdy, children. The youngest pulls my tail, thinking it's a snake. Hello? Snakes don't swish and show their mood! The others stroke my fur the wrong way, so I look like I've been in a fight with one of those horrible alley cats who have no manners and lick their tails at their milk bowl. Disgusting, I call it.

My owners (what owners? I own myself!) don't let me in until that contraption of theirs 'dongs' eight times. Even then she insists on brushing me until all my fur comes out. How am I supposed to look thirty? She makes me look fifty! Humans have this problem so why doesn't she, of all people, appreciate it?

Well, rather than sitting under this big machine that roars, I'll go in. Today I'll hide so she can't sigh about my hair loss. I'd dye it, but I'm a cat. Ever operated a bottle with paws? Talk about a nightmare!

Renu Kumar (11)

TWO THINGS TO FIND

One Christmas, Rebecca and Louise were running downstairs to see if Father Christmas had been. He had. They ran towards the fire and got their stockings. After opening the presents out of their stockings, they found out they'd got a chocolate bar, a book and lots more.

When they had played with their toys, they rushed to the Christmas tree. The first present they opened was a book, it was an old and tatty book. They opened the book and it was hollow. Suddenly, they were pulled in to the book. They whirled around. Soon, they heard a voice saying, 'You only have one day to find two things. You have to find an ink pot and an old quill.'

Suddenly, they were shooting out of a post box. They decided to get on, because they only had one day to find the ink pot and pen.

After ten minutes, they saw a little kid with a bag. She looked like she was going to school. They decided to follow her. They walked for three minutes, they were still not there, so they spoke to her. They said, 'Where are you going?'
'I am going to school,' she replied.
Rebecca asked, 'How long is it?'
'There it is,' she said, pointing to a big building.

After one minute they were there. As they walked into the school, they saw a spare ink pot and a quill. 'Yes!'
Rebecca looked at her watch. They rushed out. They took four minutes to get back to the post box. Soon they were at the post box. They jumped into the post box and the same voice who spoke earlier said, 'Well done.'

'We're back at home and Mum is still in bed!'

Charlotte Morgan (9)
Bardsey Primary School

THE TUDOR HOLIDAY

It was Saturday morning and the Williams were getting ready to go on holiday. They were really happy because they had not been on holiday for ages. Emma was even more excited, because it was her birthday. She was going to be nine. On the way, Emma was a bit of a nuisance because every five minutes, she would say, 'Are we there yet?' or 'Are we nearly there, Mum?'

When they got there, Emma was not very happy because it was too hot. Her mum and dad really liked Italy and ran into the hotel. Emma asked if she could go to the museum and look at the paintings. So after they finished unpacking, they got in the car and started driving. When they got there, Emma ran inside. She really liked the Tudors because she was studying them, so she wanted to find a painting of Henry VIII.
'Emma, Emma,' called a voice. It was Mum, running up to Emma. Emma touched the painting of Henry VIII safely and slowly.

Suddenly, out shot a great big man with velvet, silk and wool all over him. Mum, Dad and Emma pushed Henry VIII back in, but fell in with him. They were back in time. Mum wasn't very happy, but Dad and Emma were. Mum wasn't very good at having fun. Mum, Dad and Emma tried to get out, but realised they had to find Henry VIII to get out.

Eventually they found him and got out of there. Emma's parents were not in a very good mood, so Emma decided it wouldn't be a good time to ask them if she could have a brother or sister.

Heléna Kilroy (9)
Bardsey Primary School

THE LAMBORGHINI RUSH

In Italy, there was a man called Vin Diesel. He was going to have a very strange day.

It was a normal day; hot, boring and tiring, but this was going to be no normal day. The president had been caught. They tied him up and left him in a Lamborghini with a bomb inside. They had put petrol all around the car. The explosion was going to go off in an hour. But the president's agent, Vin Diesel, was on the case.

He was in his Ferrari GTO and zooming down the road and he was going at 120mph. He was only over the speed limit a little bit! He was now only half an hour away when he saw a wall of cops! He put his foot down and *bang!* There was a massive cloud of smoke and a shower of metal.

The Ferrari flew out! There were more cops and one of them rammed him off the road. But he carried on. He was driving for about ten minutes when he came to a car park. He saw the Lamborghini parked there. He got out of his car and ran over to the Lamborghini. There he saw the man with the match. He ran over to the guy and hit the match out of his hand. There was a sudden silence as the match fell, then there was a massive explosion. The president and his agent though, had got to shelter and were fine.

Oliver Frankel (9)
Bardsey Primary School

THE FORGOTTEN ISLAND

John and his dad were on their way to Africa. They looked out of the window of the plane and saw the wing was breaking and the plane was beginning to spin. Suddenly, it shot down towards the ground like a bullet. John and his dad quickly pulled the eject lever and shot out of the plane. They fell through the clouds slowly and steadily.

Just then, John saw an island. He showed his dad and they directed their parachutes to the island. When they landed, they saw the plane fall through the clouds and into the water with a humungous splash. John and his dad knew that nobody else survived, so they walked further into the jungle. Soon, nightfall came so they decided to make camp.

In the morning, they talked about how they were going to get off the island. After about a week of muddy clothes and cut knees, they had built a raft and soon they set off. After about three hours, John saw smoke in the distance. As they got closer, they realised it was a ship. The ship took them back to England and they lived happily ever after.

Jamie Hammond (9)
Bardsey Primary School

LAUREN'S ADVENTURE

I couldn't get to sleep. I was too excited. It was my birthday the next day. I was too busy thinking about what I would get. Would it be a book, or a new dress?

Suddenly, it was morning. I rushed downstairs into the kitchen. Mum was baking a cake, it smelt gorgeous and freshly baked. 'Mmm, smells good.'
Mum turned around shocked. 'I didn't know you were there,' said Mum. 'You surprised me.'
'Sorry,' I giggled.
'Happy birthday,' said Dad. 'Your presents are over in the corner.'
I quickly opened my first present. Inside was my favourite band's new album. I opened my next present in the flowery wrapping paper. Inside was a pair of trainers and a pair of 'Hello Kitty' socks. I opened the rest of my presents. My favourite present was the new Harry Potter book.
'Do you want to go to the fair now?' asked Mum.
'OK,' I said.

When we were there, I went on the ghost train. There were lots of ghosts around. One caught my attention, he climbed in the train. I said I would meet my mum at the park.

Me and Jake (that was what the ghost said his name was) went on an adventure all around. We went on a roller coaster and we got stuck. Just then, the ghost turned bad. I screamed and woke up. It was all a dream!

Olivia Dalrymple (8)
Bardsey Primary School

WITCH GOES DOWN

In the flower garden, it was Christmas. The snow lay flat and nicely along the ground and it glittered. Big, small and tiny animals of all different kinds were eating Christmas dinner.
'Yum-yum,' baby Lucy said in a sweet tweet.
Boom! Boom!
'Zoe and Chloe,' Mum yelled, 'get down here.'
The Bird family sat around the table eventually, when Chloe and Zoe had come.

Suddenly, Barn Owl and Wise Owl flew across the house and dropped a big parcel. As the parcel lay flat, it gave a ruffle.
Boom! The Bird family had gone.

They awoke lying on a dusty floor. The big house nest had fallen. They were now in a dark, gloomy castle. Somebody was dropping things into a big bowl.
'I know what that is,' yelled Zoe, 'it's a cauldron.'
'Shhhh,' they whispered.
The baby screamed, 'A baby fairy!'
The Bird family looked gloomy and then saw more fairies.
A croaky voice yelled, 'I am ruined!' She fell to the ground and all that was left was clothes.

The Bird family woke again and the nest was still ruined, but it had all been a dream. So they built a new nest. This one was better.

It was soon spring. Flowers, leaves and grass were back. The new nest never fell and years went by. No problems came. Mum, Rachel, Dad and the baby sunbathed, when more booms came. They realised people were moving in and out, and so made and lost friends.

Fine years went by, They were happy for a long time.

Rhian Miles (9)
Bardsey Primary School

POWDER TINY

My cat, Scary and I were working on a project. We had to make an orange squeezer. I only had to make the power work and it would be finished. I was swapping some wires and putting some powder in, when I spilled it all over my face. Scary touched my leg and my whole body began shrinking. I decided to get one of the small ladders I had invented last year. Because I couldn't carry it, Scary helped me up.

It was the big day, the orange squeezer was in the big hall just next to the school. It was marked number 10. They would be judging it in about half an hour. I couldn't make an unshrinking potion, but maybe I could find one.

I searched around the hall. I thought I could stand under a potion and it would turn me the right size, because I was too small. It was one minute until they judged. I was right under a potion, when a boy dropped it on me. They were just about to put fourth prize on my orange squeezer, when I started to get bigger, and bigger, and bigger. They spotted me and swapped fourth to first prize for the best growing ever. I had a maximum of £110,000 to spend on something I really, really wanted.

I bought an orange squeezer!

Lauren Blackburn (9)
Bardsey Primary School

THE LAMBORGHINI RUSH

Last year, Vin Diesel was in a rush trying to find the Lamborghini with the Queen inside it. He was trying to get to his destination fast because the Queen was tied up and there was petrol all around the car she was in. It wasn't that easy because terrorists were guarding it. To get to the car park, Vin Diesel had to really put his foot down on the accelerator because he had a time limit of one hour to get to the Queen, or *bang!* Vin Diesel was in a Ferrari GTO, so it was very fast.

Vin had to go along the motorway. He was going at 126mph, so he was breaking the speed limit a lot. The police were right behind him, but he didn't stop, he just kept going even faster. Vin Diesel was the Queen's agent and was on the case.

Vin spotted a race that was just about to start. He still had fifty minutes left, so he raced in his Ferrari. (If you won, you won three thousand pounds). Vin Diesel had a struggle at first, but then he got the hang of it. Vin won and got a new turbo, and as he got back on the road, he saw a great big wall of cars. The cars were cop cars. He just put his foot down, when suddenly a great big cloud of smoke arose. Now there were more police cars behind him.
One of the policemen shouted in his car, 'Pull over, maniac.'

Vin Diesel got to the car park and ran up and hit all the terrorists over the head. He soon found the Lamborghini, but before Vin could get away, the match fell on the petrol and so the car was surrounded by fire. Vin revved the car to make some of the fire blow out. He then saved the Queen and drove out. Soon, he heard a great big *bang!* But everyone was safe. Mission completed.

Oliver Eastman (9)
Bardsey Primary School

THE CREEPY CUPBOARD

One spooky night, three children were walking out on the street. They were called Chris, Hannah and William. As they were walking, they found a cupboard door stuck onto a brick wall.
'This wasn't here before,' said William.
Soon they dared each other to open the cupboard door that had never been opened before.

They were about to open it when William got scared and he burst into tears. Chris and Hannah had never seen him so scared. So they opened it on their own. Then a ghost chased them to Chris' house. They were fast and managed to escape.

The next night, they went back to open the door, but it was not there. Where was it?

Christopher Ham (8)
Bardsey Primary School

MY ADVENTURE STORY

One beautiful day I was very excited because me and my two friends, Frances and Georgia, were all going on an adventure and my mum and dad were not coming. We took a spade and my mum kindly dropped us off at the caves and so the adventure started.

We had to climb the cave because we could not get in the bottom. As we reached inside the cave, there in front of us appeared the most enormous bear in the world. We ran out and down the cave as fast as we could go, otherwise I think we would have been his dinner.

This time when we went up the cave, we went all the way up and at the top found a big red cross, so I got the spade and started to dig. We soon found gold and treasure and we ran home as fast as we could go and showed Mum.

When my mum saw, she was amazed and she said, 'Well done.' And we too said, 'Well done,' to ourselves. It was the best day ever.

Hannah Sheerin (8)
Bardsey Primary School

ME AND MY WITCH

One sunny day, my mum decided that we had to move because we didn't have enough bedrooms. I felt sad leaving. We got ready to pack up. When we'd packed, we moved in and got everything ready and put it in the right places. When we'd settled down, I said, 'Why did we have to leave home?' and then I started to cry.
'Cheer up, it's not the end of the world,' said Mum.

I slowly walked up the stairs. I lay down on my bed and I fell asleep. Suddenly, I heard a laughing noise. I opened my eyes and found it was a person who had got an enormous wart on her nose. It was a witch! I screamed really loudly.
'Charlotte, what is the matter with you today?' shouted Mum.
'There's a witch in my bedroom. (The witch had now disappeared.) It's true.'
'Get to sleep now,' said Mum.
'OK.'

Soon, there it was again, the witch was back.
'Hello,' it looked at me.
'What are you doing in my bedroom?' I said.
'I live here, of course,' it said and left.

It was finally morning and I went to school, but I kept the witch a secret. After school, I went to my bedroom and said, 'You can come out now. What is your name?'
'My name is Wendy, the witch.'
'Will you come to my party on Saturday 27th July at 8pm?' I said.
'Wait, I've got some friends who are living in the toilet.'
'Who are they?'
'They are Jewel, Diamond and Crown.'

On Saturday, they set off to the party (and the party wasn't just a party, it was a wicked party). They trapped me and my friends told of her friends and the witch saved us. That's how we made friends.

But then there was another noise. I wonder what that noise is? *Argh!*

Megan Marshall (8)
Bardsey Primary School

THE TUDOR ADVENTURE

Louise and Ashley jumped into the car to go to the museum. Mum picked up the picnic box and she climbed into the car. Dad drove us to the museum. We jumped out of the car and walked into the museum.
'It is so cool,' said Ashley.
They looked at the old Tudor clothes and at an old house. Then they found an old chest. It was really cool. Ashley and Louise opened the door and stepped inside. Soon they started falling down and down. When they finally got to the bottom, they realised they were in Tudor times. It was so weird. They walked further into the Tudor town, when they saw a clothes shop and a food shop. They soon found their house. They went in. Mum and Dad were there, they realised they were Tudor people. They played in town all day long and had great fun. After, they had tea.

The next morning, they went to a furniture shop where they found another chest. Louise and Ashley stepped inside and fell down, then *bang!* They were at the bottom of the chest and were back at the Tudor museum.

Mum was shouting, 'Louise and Ashley, it's dinner time.'

After dinner, they walked further into the museum. They looked at a picture of King Henry VIII.

At the end of the day, they got into the car. It took ages to get home.

Hannah Donaghy (9)
Bardsey Primary School

DIARY

Dear Diary,

Today was the best day in my whole, entire life! Me and my family went to Blackpool Pleasure Beach, and the rides were amazing! I went on nearly all the rides and they were all great.

First we went to the box office and got fast-track tickets for £36 each (it was well worth it). Then we went on the first ride which was the roller coaster, it was really smooth and fun. Next, we went on the Grand National. It was similar to the roller coaster, but much bumpier. Then we went on loads of other rides, they were really cool!

Later, me and my dad went on the Pepsi Max, the biggest and best ride! I was really nervous about going on it and didn't want to at first, but when I was on it, I really, really enjoyed it! I wanted to go on it again, but it was lunchtime.

After lunch, we waited for a while and then went on nearly all the rides again, and I went on the Pepsi Max loads of times. But then it was getting dark and we needed to go home. I will never forget that day!

Rachel Bonney (11)
Bardsey Primary School

A Dream Interview With Kylie

Me: Hi, Kylie, and thank you for sparing your time to come on the show to talk to us.

Kylie: That's OK!

Me: So, what got you into music then?

Kylie: Well, it isn't really an answer, but I have been singing ever since I was little with my younger sister, but I don't know really. Well, I guess I just didn't want to be normal, I wanted to make a difference in myself.

Me: Great, but now your little sister's taken it up too, how do you feel about this? Do you feel jealous in any way?

Kylie: No, not at all, I'm pleased for her in the same way as she was pleased for me and it's a huge step for her!

Me: Over the years, we've seen you move on from the good show 'Neighbours', then we had Holly Valance and recently, now, Delta Goodrem! How do you feel about this?

Kylie: I feel fine with it, they've come a long way!

Me: Here's a question I've always wanted to ask you, do you think you deserved for two years winning the award for best female singer?

Kylie: I'm not being boastful or anything, but yeah, I do!

Me: Simple question, why?

Kylie: Well look, I've been doing this for 10-11 years, so I think I deserve any trophies or awards that come my way.

Me: Now how long are you expecting to carry one, what are your targets for the future?

Kylie: Well, I hope to settle down quite soon.

Me: Thank you for coming to talk to us!

Kylie: It's nothing.

Me: Bye, Kylie.

Kylie: Thank you, bye.

Deborah Todd (11)
Bardsey Primary School

A Day In The Life Of A Millionaire

I woke up as usual in my luxury penthouse suite. I came into my walk-in wardrobe and spent ages picking out the perfect outfit. Today I was going on holiday to Menorca! I ran downstairs and got my breakfast, brushed my teeth, got washed and got in my Saab convertible to drive to the airport.

I arrived at Leeds and Bradford Airport. I was half an hour early, so I had plenty of time to look around the shops. I texted Amy, my friend, who I was going on holiday with saying, 'R U amost @ the airport?' She texted me back saying, 'I'm nearly there, CU soon.'
I bought a pair of Calvin Klein flip-flops and sat on a chair by a café.

Amy arrived and we heard the speakers above saying, 'The gate to Mahon Airport is now open.' So we rushed to the gate, got outside and onto the plane. I really couldn't wait to swim, relax, have fun and shop!

Stephanie Douglas (11)
Bardsey Primary School

DIARY

Dear Diary,

Today was really nice, you see my family and I went to the beach at Cayton Bay. It was hot and the sun was shining. When we arrived, we got an ice cream. I got a Galaxy one, it was really yum! We walked down to the beach. By the time we were there, our ice creams were finished. Because I had my swimming costume on and my dad had his swimming shorts on, we both put on our snorkels and went into the sea.

The sea was quite warm and very calm. My dad said to me, 'Shall we go look for some fish?' I said yes, so we did.

Me and my dad were swimming along when we found the most beautiful fish ever. It was yellow and black striped, with big gleaming eyes. We thankfully brought the underwater camera with us, so we took a couple of photos of it. Then we went to look at the other fish. Me and my dad took it in turns to take pictures. We had taken as many as we could and played with the fish until it was time for lunch. We got out of the sea and walked over to lunch.

For lunch, I had a ham baguette with salad and finished off with prawn cocktail crisps and a Dairy Milk chocolate bar. My mum and dad had the same as me, and my brothers had a tuna baguette, some crisps and a Yorkie each.

After lunch, we played a bit of football. The teams were me and Dad, and the other team was my mum and two brothers. After that, it was time to go home. It was getting quite late, so we went back to the car and set off. *That was a brill day!*

Love, Lucy.

Lucy Beddard (11)
Bardsey Primary School

DIARY OF TRACY BEAKER

26/6/03
Dear Diary,

I haven't written in you in ages. Anyway, this new girl came today called Justine. What a name! Justine Littlewood. She only came because her mum left and her dad had to look after four kids. He couldn't cope, so he put Justine in care, her two brothers went to a different home.

I can't believe that Louise. Just because I called Justine a cry baby, Louise called me horrible and now they're best friends. Justine's dad was supposed to come last Saturday, but he never turned up, so she's now in a big strop. She didn't even turn up for breakfast. Louise came to breakfast, but didn't sit in her normal place next to me, all because of what I called Justine!

See you tomorrow.

26/6/03
It's me again. I'm in a good mood today because I got a letter from Sam! She says I can help her to do a story because she likes my pictures and writing. Me and Sam are having a special day out next Saturday. I don't know where we're going, but it has to be good!

Today, wimpy Peter Ingham asked me to play with him. I did because I had nothing else to do! We played things like hangman and noughts and crosses. It was only good because I won all the time!

Peter isn't that bad, but now I've played with him he thinks we're the best friends ever.

I'll write back soon.
Love from,
Tracy Beaker.

Jessica Procter (11)
Bardsey Primary School

A Day In The Life Of A Baby

Today was amazing! My mummy gave me two bottles of milk instead of one. Hey, guess what? I got another new mum again! This one wears sparkly jeans and a pink top, unlike my old one. She wore a blue top.

We went to the park in the village. I felt so grown up as I got to go on the big girls' swing. It as really scary. I actually moved! You had to hold on very tight, or you'd fall off!

When I had been in the tunnel, which my mum called a 'Don't be silly, that's a drainpipe,' my mum went to the ''air dresser's'. My mum sat in the seat, but out came a second new mum. This one had short, highlighted hair.

It's my birthday on May 15th! Only three days. I am growing up! Now I can eat a whole yoghurt. I can't wait!

Lucy Nunn (11)
Bardsey Primary School

A Day In The Life Of My Friend Molly

8.45am
I am woken up by Harry. He is whining as per usual. This time it's about waking up early. I went downstairs and sat down at the table.
'What's for breakfast, Mum?' I asked.
'Bacon sandwich.'
After breakfast, I went to get ready for Japanese school.

9.30am
When I arrive, Lucy is waiting for me. Our first lesson is writing out the last bit of a story.

10am
I finished the story and it is time for art. Today we are painting plates in a Japanese theme.

11.30am
Break time!

12.15pm
Lunch. Today I have tuna pasta, French bread and a chocolate bar. Lucy just came and sat down next to me.

1pm
I'm off to the cinema with Natalie, Ellie and Lucy. We are going to see 'Maid in Manhattan'.

3pm
'Maid in Manhattan' was really good. Now we are off to McDonald's for tea. As usual, we all have a Happy Meal.

4pm
I'm back home now and getting ready to go to Ellie's house for a sleepover, but before that, I'm gonna have a rest.

Elysa Manning (11)
Bardsey Primary School

AN INTERVIEW WITH JACQUELINE WILSON

Me: Here is Galaxy 105 in the morning with the beautiful Lisa Galinsky and in the studio today, we have one of the best-selling children's authors, Jacqueline Wilson.

Jacqueline: Hello Galaxy!

Me: So Jacqueline, how do you feel about being one of the best-selling authors?

Jacqueline: Great, but it's quite hard writing all those books.

Me: I know how you feel. So, how many books have you actually written?

Jacqueline: About 18, but I've lost count.

Me: Wow! What a lot of books! Now Jacqueline, I know this is hard, but which, out of all your books, is your favourite?

Jacqueline: It's really hard to say, but I like 'The Story Of Tracy Beaker' because it was the first book I wrote that was published.

Me: Now that's all we've got time for! You can catch me, Lisa Galinsky, in the morning on Galaxy 105. Thanks Jacqueline!

Jacqueline: Any time.

Lisa Galinsky (11)
Bardsey Primary School

A Diary All About Me

'Jennifer, wake up.'
It's my mum, she wants me to get up and help her make my costume. At school, we're performing 'Oliver', I'm starring as Widow Corney. All of my friends are in it and we're going to be so good. My mum feels really bad because she can't come to see it, so she's trying to be really nice to me to make up for not being there. It's really cool having a slave.

So back to making my costume. I've got to make a big skirt and a nice top which is really frilly and cool. My mum might have to make the skirt a bit smaller because it is really big and long. I will look really good.

Two days later...

I've just got back from performing 'Oliver' and it went really, really well. Everyone was stunning and we all looked amazing.

Jennifer Smith (11)
Bardsey Primary School

A Day In The Life Of A Superstar

Bring, bring! That was my alarm clock telling me I've got to get up to start the busy, hectic day that's ahead of me. So I slipped some clothes on and went down to get my breakfast. Just something like a banana.

I called my limo to come and take me down to the studio. I had an appointment to record my third album called 'Walking Around With Three legs'. This took three hours. It always does, especially when I'm in a rush. It took three hours again today because I had vocal training. I always do this 'cause I'm getting old and I need to see if my vocals are still as good as they used to be.

I popped in to Betty's for lunch, sat in my special chair which I always sit in and looked at my watch. I realised I had my sister, Steph, coming over for tea, so I rushed to Sainsbury's in my Ferrari and bought a few bits and bobs. I was going to make lasagne and have red wine to drink. I hope she'll enjoy it. I haven't seen her since I was 11!

In the middle of making the dinner, I got a phone call from the studio saying the recording machine was broken, so I had to go tomorrow and record it again! I put that behind me and carried on making tea.

Ding-dong, Steph was here. We had a lovely evening watching films and she went home at 1.30am! Finally now, it's bedtime!

Amy Robertson (11)
Bardsey Primary School

My Spooky House

One evening I was having tea and it was late, so I had to go to bed. I shouted, *'Help!'* because a ghost had appeared in my bedroom. I shouted to my mum first, but she didn't hear me, so quietly I got into bed. The whole night I couldn't get to sleep. I told the ghost over and over again to be quiet, but it would not stop banging around.

Finally, I shouted for Mum again, but she did not hear me, so I went downstairs for some help.
'There is a ghost in my bedroom,' I said to Mum in a raised voice.
'I don't believe you,' said my mother.
So I told my dad, but he didn't believe me either, so I went upstairs and had to put up with the ghost.

Finally I got to sleep. When I woke up, I looked in the corner and the ghost was still there. 'Go away, ghost!' I shouted. 'You don't scare me.' Then it went away and I began cheering.
My mum came in and said, 'What are you doing?' Mum was shouting because I was shaking the ceiling by jumping for joy.

Rebecca Holder (8)
Bardsey Primary School

THE MAGIC BOOK

I heard a story from my grandma about a girl who saw an angel once, but now my grandma has died. Then last night, when I was asleep, I saw a strange light from the book my grandma had read from. I was scared to open it, but my grandma once told me that I have a lion's heart, so I opened it.

There I saw my grandma. She was dressed as a queen. Suddenly, one of the guards pulled me in the book. I was scared, but my grandma said to me, 'Julie, you are a princess.'
'I . . . I can't be a princess!'
'But you are Julie, and this is your palace.'
'Then, if I'm a princess, then that means . . .'
'Yes, all your family are royalty.'
I couldn't say a thing, so my grandma said, 'Put on these clothes.'
'How do you put on these clothes?'
'I will tell you,' said Grandma.

Then I woke up. I realised it was all a dream, but it felt so real. When I later looked at the book, I saw that the pictures moved. Then I knew it was real.

Ifsa Hussain (11)
Boothroyd J&I School

FIRE AT BOOTHROYD

'Have you brought your history homework, Ahsan?' said Arfan.
There was Haseen and Aqib.
'Oh crap, I've forgotten it five times this week, now it's home time detention for all next week!'
'I love to watch you get in trouble - best time for me,' laughed Dan, his worst enemy.
Then they slowly, slowly walked to their classes. They had history first lesson, where they had to give in their work. They walked quite slowly, Ahsan was going to stay out of school till the first lesson ended. As he was going to do it, Arfan, Haseen and Aqib stopped him from going out of school.
Mr Latham shouted, 'Where are you going? You should be in your history lesson. Please check your timetable, you should go to Mrs Smith's class. You've been here long enough to know your timetable.'

Mrs Smith said, 'Ahsan, come here and hand your homework in.'
Ahsan said, 'Miss, I lost my homework in the park when I was playing.'
Mrs Smith was very angry and said, 'Do your work after school in detention.'
Ahsan didn't go to his detention and ran off home.

The next day when he arrived at school, the teacher said, 'I have sent a letter home to your parents and you will be in big trouble.'
Haseen said to Miss, 'Please can I go to the toilet?'
The teacher said, 'Yes, go on, but be quick.'
But Haseen didn't go to the toilet, he went to the changing rooms, got a lighter and took out a cigarette and tried to light it up. He smoked a bit and didn't like it, so he threw it in the bin, walked out and put chewing gum in his mouth.
When he went back, the teacher said, 'Where have you been for such a long time?'
Haseen said, 'I had diarrhoea.'
The teacher said, 'You have diarrhoea in all of my lessons.'
Haseen said, 'Yes.'

As soon as he said yes, the fire bell rang and all the class lined up to go out. When they lined up outside, Mrs Smith sent Arfan to get the register. When he came back, the fire officers were there.

They said, 'Somebody started a fire in the changing rooms by a cigarette. We will find out who it is and they will have to pay a fine.'

Mrs Smith knew it was Haseen, as he was the only one out of class. Mr Ford shouted at him and sent him home with a letter telling his parents they would have to pay a big fine. Haseen was really sorry about what he did and said he would not do anything wrong again.

Harun Nawaz (8)
Boothroyd J&I School

The Old School

It was pouring down when it was home time and Claire had to walk home in it because her mum was working and her father was shopping down town. As the bell went and the children left the classroom, Claire realised she didn't have a coat, because it was in the wash. As soon as Claire walked out of the school building, she was soaked. Everyone had gone, except the teachers who were busy setting work out for the next school day. Claire walked past the old school, the gates were squeaking and crashing. Just at that moment, the rain got faster and faster. Claire had to find shelter, but where? Then Claire noticed the old school door was unlocked, so she hurried inside.

The building looked strange compared to the school that had just been built. The old school had lots and lots of cobwebs. Claire heard quite a lot of moaning, so she felt very uncomfortable. The old school smelt rotten. Suddenly, there was a mighty *bang*. Claire jumped in horror, but it was only the wind blowing the rusty door shut. Then something black scurried across the floor. It was a rat.

It then turned half-past three and Claire's mum would have come home from work wondering where her daughter was, so Claire took out her mobile and tried ringing her mum, but there was no signal. Claire heard another rustling noise, but this time it wasn't a rat, it was something more creepy, something that was watching Claire's every move, something that might hurt her if she shrieked. All she could do was stand still and keep quiet.

Then the figure went away, but Claire didn't know where. She had to find it. She had to know what the creature was and how dangerous it was. Claire walked on down the wooden corridor and into an old science lab. There she found a signal on the phone. She stayed in the science lab wondering if she should phone her mum or keep her investigation a secret. Then she heard a beep, it was her phone. She had a message, she read it but the message wasn't from her mum, it was from someone in the school. It said, *'Leave, danger coming, leave!'* Once more Claire jumped back in horror. She knew someone was in this school, but who knew her?

Claire decided to go and find out who this mystery person or creature was, and why they were in the old school. She once more stepped into the wooden corridor and made her way to the staircase. The staircase was falling apart. Claire didn't want to go to the top of them, but she had to. She carefully put her feet on the treads, hoping they would hold her weight. Finally, Claire reached to top of the battered staircase. The second floor had rubble everywhere, but that wasn't bothering her now. She had the feeling that something was watching her again. This time she was going to move, she wasn't going to be scared. As she moved, something jumped down in front of her. Claire gasped, 'Who are you and what do you want?'

'Freedom,' the thing replied, then it stepped into the light. The thing that Claire wanted to meet was her old best friend, Sarah, who was meant to have moved house. She had loads of scratches and dry blood on her face. What could Claire do? Should she run away or stay? What do you think?

Hannah Wilson (10)
Boothroyd J&I School

ADAM'S JOURNEY

For Adam, it was a day worth waiting for. As he saw the rain outside, he thought to himself, *I can't wait for sun, sun, sun in Pakistan!* When he remembered coming home from school one day and his parents telling him he was going to Pakistan, he still couldn't believe how badly he had behaved, like a spoilt brat. Thankfully now, Adam had realised how lucky he was to go to Pakistan, especially with his cousins.

When Adam got downstairs, he saw his mother doing her last minute packing. She looked worried. He thought about helping her, but today he wasn't going to do anything but relax. The clock struck nine o'clock, finally it was time to go. 'Can we go now?' he asked his mother.
'Yes,' she replied.
Adam ran out of the door and got in the car. It took ages for his mother to lock the door and check it was locked.

Two hours later, Adam woke up in the car to see all his relatives looking at him. 'What are you looking at?' he asked.
'You,' said one of his cousins.
Then his sister said, 'You snore.'
'No I don't,' Adam replied.
After that, Adam waited with his family for an hour to get on the plane. Then he, his mother, aunt, uncle and cousins said goodbye to the rest of his family and gave their tickets to a woman.

By this time, Adam felt very confused as he'd never been to an airport before. At last he was outside the aeroplane. He looked up and said, 'Man, this is massive.'
His mother asked him, 'Which 'man' are you talking about?'
Adam said, 'You know what I mean, Mum!'

On the plane, Adam was given a seat with his favourite cousin, Kaleem. The food the air hostess gave them was disgusting. 'The next time I go on an aeroplane,' he said to his cousin, 'I will go on a jet by first class!'

'How are you going to afford that?' Kaleem asked.
'Er, I'm going to be rich!' said Adam.
Kaleem shook his head and said, 'No, I am going to be rich first. I'll buy you a ticket on a jet. I've got a business plan and a bank account. You haven't got either!'
They both laughed about their dreams.
They landed in Pakistan hours later and Adam's grandad was waiting for them. They were going to stay with him and his wife, who was Adam's step-grandma.

At Adam's grandparents' house, he ate and went to bed. In all the time Adam had been in Pakistan, he'd never had a good night's sleep.

While Adam was in Pakistan, he made friends with their neighbours who had a very big house, that was all he remembered about them. During most of the days, Adam and his cousins played in the garden or watched 'Mr Bean'. In Pakistan, the most exciting thing to do there was to ride on a motorbike in the water. After, he remembered the motorbike ride as the most exciting thing he'd done in his life.

When it was time to go home, Adam was happy to go home. This was because he'd been in Pakistan for three months and he missed his family. The plane ride went quicker than Adam thought it would. When he saw his dad at Manchester Airport, he was so happy, he hugged him. His father drove them home, then went to Bradford to have a little celebration. Then they went home for a good sleep, the first in a long time.

Akeel Javid (9)
Boothroyd J&I School

A Day In The Life Of Gareth Gates

One sunny morning, a limo pulled up outside Gareth Gates' mansion, while he was having bacon and eggs for his breakfast.

He got in the limo and went to Sheffield to do a concert. When he got there, there were fans waiting outside for him shouting, 'Gareth we love you,' and 'Gareth, can we have your autograph?' Gareth gave them his autograph and then went inside to his dressing room to get ready for the concert.

At 5 o'clock, Gareth was on stage singing all his songs. People had signs saying, *I Love You Gareth.*
I passed out because he was so good, then I had to go to hospital. Gareth came to see me and asked me if I would like to come to the mansion.

So the next week, I went to his mansion and had a cup of tea and talked about what had happened at the concert. I told him I was feeling much better. He then gave me his autograph and we said goodbye and I was taken home in his limo.

Jodi Hartley (11)
Fairburn CP School

SCOOBY-DOO AND THE HAUNTED HOUSE

It was a cold day. Shaggy, Scrappy and Scooby were going down a country lane when, *bang!* 'Argh,' shouted Shaggy, 'we're gonna die.' They had a puncture in their back tyre. As soon as the mystery machine stopped shaking, they all got out. They had stopped next to a big and scary-looking house.
'Relp!' shouted Scooby. 'I'm not going in.'
As Scrappy and Shaggy came out of the mystery machine, Scrappy said, 'Yes you are,' and he lifted Shaggy and Scooby and took them into the big house.

When the gang got in the house, they started to look around. At the first hallway, Shaggy decided to go left. As they approached the door, they were dreading to open it.

Meanwhile, Scrappy was looking through all the rooms. When he reached the room where Scooby and Shaggy were, he barged through. In the room was food and lots of it, so they ate and ate. Then all of a sudden, '*Ooooooh!*' came a muffled voice.
'Relp! There's a ghost!' shouted Scooby. 'Let's get out of here.'

So they ran like the wind, changed their tyre and drove away.

Thomas William Hetherington (11)
Fairburn CP School

EGGY SURPRISE

Hi, my name is Tania Fluffell. I have blonde hair, so people think that I am dizzy and stupid. That really gets on my nerves. Though the thing that bothers me the most is George Stuffman. Even Jessie Dann, my best friend agrees with me and Jessie is the kindest person ever.

It all started when we heard a noise at school. We could hear it coming from the cellar. It was a sort of banging noise. As the kind people that we are, we decided to go and see if anyone was in trouble (we wanted the gossip too!)

As we crept down the gloomy staircase, we spotted three perfect eggs in a neat row.
'I wonder if we should move them?' Jessie asked.
'I'm not so sure . . . what if an alien put them there. What if . . . ?'
'George Stuffman,' we agreed together in chorus.

We both stopped and stared in shock as the three eggs suddenly cracked. What was happening? The next thing that happened was probably the worst thing that has happened to us in our lives (well, except when we both fell headfirst into a smelly ditch!) Three George Stuffmans formed from the yolk in the smooth eggs and the shell vanished! Just like that, we had three copies of our worst enemy standing before our very eyes.
'Er, Jessie . . .' I started, but before I could finish, the three robots twisted into the shape of Jessie. 'I guess these aren't so bad after all!'

Hayley Rhodes (11)
Fairburn CP School

A Day In The Life Of Piper Hallawell

I'm running. I don't know where to, but I don't know what to do! Prue had killed herself for the world! She's gone and can't come back. Oh how will Phoebe and Leo take it?

I'm in the woods, it's dark and gloomy and also cold. Why did this happen to me? Who was that? I have just heard someone. It sounds like two people and they're coming my way. It's a man and a woman! I've got to hide but I can't, I'm paralysed to the spot! Oh no, it's Phoebe and Leo, they must have come to find me. I can see them and they can also see me.
'Piper, thank goodness you're here!' Phoebe exclaimed, giving me a big hug.
'Piper, are you hurt? Because if you are, I can heal you with my Lightwhiter powers. You don't look it, so why are you crying?' Leo said, looking worried.
'Where's Prue, Piper? She won't answer her cell,' Phoebe asked.
'She isn't here,' I said, wonderingly.
'Where is she then? When will she be back?'
'She can't come back, she's gone.'
'Do you mean dead?' Leo asked, shocked.
'Yes, she has gone away forever. She died for the world.' Phoebe burst into tears.
'What will we do now? Will you lose your powers seeing as the Power of the Charmed Ones has been broken?' Leo asked sadly.
'No, because we'll call Paige, our other younger sister!'

Laura Coldwell (11)
Fairburn CP School

THE MYSTERY OF THE MISSING EASTER EGG

One morning I woke up, I was looking forward to my Easter egg. I fed my rabbit, then I had a look for my Easter egg. I found a small one, but that wasn't it because my mum said there was a big one somewhere. I looked all over the house. I looked in the kitchen and in the living room. I looked in my mum's bedroom, even in my bedroom. I became sad because I could not find my Easter egg, so I went into the kitchen to get a drink. My head was droopy, but then I saw footprints, no, rabbit prints. I looked out of the window and they led to the hutch, so I wondered if Blossom had pinched it.

I went outside, got Blossom out, and there it was! Blossom had opened it up for me and it was yummy. Mystery solved!

Georgina Barker (8)
Fairburn CP School

MY LOVE FROM LONDON

One day, a boy from London named Milo met a girl from the country named Candy and they fell in love with each other. They went for moonlight walks and watched the sunset from the cliffs of the country together.

One day, Candy grew bored. She picked up her pink satin frilly dress and went over to Milo. He looked handsome in his outfit of white and gold. Then they looked into each other's eyes and they kissed. But then it all went wrong. Candy leapt too far and went over the cliff. Milo ran home with tears in his eyes, he really loved her.

Everyone was sad about the death of poor, sweet Candy. The next day, Milo sat on the rock thinking about Candy. Then it went dark and he saw the ghost of Candy. He jumped to be with her and that is why it is now called Lover's Cliff. They're still up there.

Stephen Lunn (10)
Fairburn CP School

HAUNTED HOUSE

On the evening of Hallowe'en night, the two twins, Hayley and Laura set out trick or treating. They were walking down Creep Street with their broomsticks, because they were witches and they had to dress up.

All of a sudden they heard a *bang!* The bang was coming through the woods, so they followed it and pushed through the trees and saw a big, spooky castle. They wobbled up to the door and there was a doorbell. Hayley put her shaking finger up to it and pressed it. There was a loud *ching, ching* noise.

Nobody answered the door, so they pushed the door and it screeched open. They heard footsteps.
Hayley said, 'Is anybody home?'
There was no answer. They saw a black-coated figure on the cobwebbed staircase. They were scared, they didn't know what to do. So they ran out of the house and rushed through the trees of the woods and saw their friends and told them all that had happened.

Hannah Langley (10)
Fairburn CP School

THE BIKE RIDE

It stood up a windy path and a steep road, its strong body carried wildlife and plants, its arms reaching out to lands over the horizon. Mount Blonket we called it. The twisting paths as well as sloping rocks made this mountain stand out from all the rest.

It was 12 o'clock at Weatherdale Activity Centre. The teacher of Group X (that was my group) bellowed in the dormitory, 'Come on, it's the bike ride. Remember to bring your gloves!' Everyone rose out of their seats and clambered out of the door. She was already there with the bikes. 'Do you want to come, X?' Every child ran, then anxiously grabbed a bike and a helmet. They mounted their bikes then shoved their helmets on.

It was an extremely nice day with the bubbling hot sun beating down on us. I knew it would be colder when we cycled up Mount Blonket. As soon as everyone was ready, we set off. The teacher told us to stay behind her at all times (but it was hard enough to keep up with her!) so I cycled my little heart out, and that was only on the windy path up to Mount Blonket. We finally reached the top and went up a hill, then we hit fresh air. As the cool, refreshing air slapped you on your cheeks, it struck you that you were in Heaven. We struggled up a slope to the steep road, and then were there. Our legs pushing, our heads sweating, I saw the top. It was only a few vertical metres up. I rode on, my head rolling, my eyes closing. I got to the top. *Victory*, there at last. I had defeated the biggest mountain I had ever seen and probably ever would see. I got a rush of blood to my head as I raced off on my bike and to the edge of the stone-cold giant. I was there where I wanted to be.

We set off to travel back. I was strangely sad to see it go. I was tired out. As I walked into the yard, a cold wind hit. I thought it was a goodbye . . . a sorry farewell.

Yasmine Crawford (11)
Farsley Farfield Primary School

THE RESIDENTIAL OF DOOM

'Is everyone here?' asked Mrs Penrice.
'I'm here!' I shouted back.
We were all really excited today, we were going on residential!

The first place we went was the big museum, it was quite fun because we could mess about without being seen! Although we didn't learn anything educational, we learnt how to roar like a bear and scare the teacher to death!

At 6.00, we arrived at the youth hostel, it was a converted church and looked very scary.
'Guess what?' shouted Edward. 'Ages ago, a plane crashed here and now it's haunted. Maybe we'll see some ghosts!'
'I hope we will!' exclaimed Beth as we walked through the little courtyard, lugging our bags behind us.

After we were all settled down in our dormitories, we were called down for tea.
'What do you think about it then?' quizzed Emma.
'I think it's a bit scary-looking . . .' Adele was suddenly interrupted by Nikki.
'Everyone listen, Becky's gone missing. I can't find her anywhere.'
'*Rah!*' shouted Kyle, making me jump. 'Maybe the ghosts have got her.'
'*Argh,*' screamed Yazzy. 'Ghosts!'
We all laughed.
'She'll turn up soon,' I said, but that was only what I hoped.

Next morning, we awoke to find Yasmine and Becky gone out of their beds. 'They're probably having their showers,' we agreed. But they weren't at breakfast either. No one seemed to notice and the teachers all had a very strange look on their faces. They didn't look awake at all!

A whole day passed and we seemed to forget about Becky. Yazzy had come back. Going back home on the coach, we never thought of Becky.

Arriving back at school, we were told some very sad and confusing news. Becky had not come on the residential, but had gone on holiday to Lanzarote. The sad news was that the plane had crashed and Becky hadn't made it. It happened the exact moment Edward told us the ghost story!

Alex Dimotsis (11)
Farsley Farfield Primary School

THE CLASSROOM MONSTER

You may have heard about scary things such as ghosts, vampires, witches and werewolves, but nothing, nothing, is as scary as . . . the classroom monster!

The gigantic, six-eyed, four-eared, green blob lives in the cupboard behind the door and he comes out when only one child is in the classroom . . . alone. Some of the kids call him Bogey Blob, but his real name is Demon.

Let me tell you the story about the little girl who forgot her apple in the classroom. She thought she would be just fine to pop in there, get it out of her lunch box and come back out. But the truth is, she never came back out. Well, she came out, but she wasn't the same girl anymore. Little Annie was such a sweet girl. She had long blonde hair always tied up in plaits and always wore a pink pinafore. But when the classroom monster got her and turned her into a demon and made her a follower of him, she even turned against her friends. She wasn't the same little Annie that everyone used to love and adore. She had really short, punky hair, and wore baggy pants and baggy T-shirts to school.

So if you don't want this to happen to you, don't ever, ever nip into the classroom alone, or else . . . the classroom monster will be *waiting!*

Danielle Hutchinson (11)
Farsley Farfield Primary School

DEADLY DEATH

Where am I? Who are you? What are you doing? *Help, help me please!* I awoke, scared and shaken from my dream. It was a nightmare. Thank goodness it was just a dream. I went downstairs to get some breakfast, then I ran to school hoping that school would take my mind off the dream.

When I got to school, we went into the hall and sat down. As the teacher was chattering on, I felt a pain in my head. Suddenly, blood started bursting out of my eyes. I started to scream. When I opened my eyes and looked, it was as if I had walked into a horror hall, it was dreadful. There were dragons everywhere, *aahhh!* It looked exactly like it had in my dream. I felt my way around the hall till I got to the door. I scrambled through the door and went to wash my face and get all the blood off.

I went back down to the hall and took a little peek, everything was back to normal. But before I went back into the hall, I asked myself, 'What made this happen, and will it happen again?'

Alex Hawkhead (8)
Farsley Farfield Primary School

THE GHOST

I was walking home on a rainy day, when the wind blew hard and blew my hat away. *Drip, drop,* went the rain heavily. Then a car drove past and sped through a puddle, my clothes got soaked. Then I noticed in front of me a girl had appeared. I looked again, but she had gone. In her place, she'd left a helmet. Inside was a spooky address, it said, '15 Cote Lane'. Then I saw the girl again. I got frightened and it was raining still. The sky was pitch-black.

I knocked on the door of 15 Cote Lane and an old man appeared. I told him the story.
Then the man went and fetched a photograph. 'Is it her?'
'Yes,' I replied.
'She's my daughter, she died ten years ago!'

Adam Choudry (9)
Farsley Farfield Primary School

THE MAGIC PENCIL CASE

One day, Tom was going to school with his pencil case in his bag, and all his homework.

He starts school at 9am. It was now 8.57, he was going to be late. He would have to hurry if he was to get there on time. Then he heard the bell go. *Uh oh,* he thought to himself. He sprinted to school. Soon he was there and boy did he feel good now he was in school. He opened his bag - horror struck him. The pens in his pencil case were tearing up his homework. 'Nooooo!' he shouted, with his head in his hands. What was he going to do? Miss Hobblenob would make him miss flying lesson and break time.

As he looked, the rubber was rubbing out the words, but the pencil wrote them back. As the compasses pierced holes and tore the sheet, the glue glued it back! He was delighted with the glue and pencil, but horrified with the compasses and rubber. When he got to class, he got very told off. Now he will never buy a pencil case again!

Mark Hodgson (9)
Farsley Farfield Primary School

TWO ADVENTUROUS GIRLS

One day, two girls went out for a walk in the dark, dark wood. Their names were Rachel and Grace. They were adventurous girls.
'The wood is very spooky tonight,' said Rachel to Grace. 'Do you want to go home, Grace?'
'No, I think it is ace.'
'I want to go home,' cried Rachel. So Rachel ran home.
'Get back here!' bellowed Grace.
'No,' replied Rachel. 'Bye, Grace,' she laughed.
'I hate you,' cried Grace.

Grace ran after her and finally she reached Rachel. She was huffing and puffing. 'R-R-Rachel, we're lost.'

'Argh!' screamed the two girls as they turned around and found a group of witches were surrounding them. They then barged through a gap and the witches soon zoomed after them. They found a tree and hid behind it.

The witches were confused.
'I will just look behind this tree,' one said.
'Uh oh, we're in trouble now,' whispered Grace.
Quickly, the two girls climbed up the tree.
'That was close,' whispered Rachel to Grace. They looked down towards the witches.
'Now they've got us,' yawned Grace.
'I'm going home, the girls have gone,' said one witch.
The witches then cackled nastily and left.
'That's strange,' said Rachel.
'Yes,' said Grace.
The two girls then crept down the tree and quietly out of the forest.

They ran all the way home. When they entered their houses, both mums shouted at them and sent them to bed, and that was the end of the two adventurous girls.

Laura McNamara (9)
Farsley Farfield Primary School

WHAT LIES IN THE CLOSET?

One dark night, it was lightning outside and Lucy was trying to get to sleep, when suddenly she heard a creaking coming from the closet. She could see it opening inch by inch, every second. Then five fat, blue fingers were sticking out, followed by a dark blue, hairy body, and then a head. He had five arms, spiky black hair and one big googly eye.

Suddenly, she heard a big, alarming noise. Lucy looked out of her window. It was her dad's car, it had been struck by lightning. She rushed into her mum and dad's room, but she was running so fast that she ran into the closet monster.

After a while of talking, they became good friends. They asked each other's names and swapped details. Lucy was no longer scared of him. They went outside to see what was the matter with the car, then they went back upstairs for a good night's sleep.

The next morning, she looked in the closet and the monster wasn't there. Lucy started to cry and she never went to sleep again.

Abigail Ramsden (9)
Farsley Farfield Primary School

THE GHOSTLY GUARDS OF DOOM ISLAND

Many years ago, there lived a group of orphans. These orphans were special because they believed in themselves and they each had a destiny. There were five of them in total and their orphan master, Mr Bittleman, was always making them work so that they could make him some money. The orphans were called Marf, Reggie, Otto, Twister and The Squidmeister. They called themselves Rocket Power Beach Bandits.

One day, Marf didn't sell any of his candy and that lost them all their TV privileges again. That was the last straw. The children made a plan that night and decided to put the plan to work straight away. The Squidmeister slowly crept into Mr Bittleman's room and turned on the PC. He hacked into the safe and stole approximately ten thousand pounds, then took the money and ran out of the fire exit.

The children slept in their little den which was under the pier and not far from the shore shack. They visited their friend Conroy, the owner of the skatepark called Madtown and he lent them some valid bus passes. They caught the bus to the beach and then they rented a jet-ski each. They started up their jet-skis and drove out to find another island.

Three or four hours later, they arrived at another island. The island was surrounded by thousands of pale, white, translucent men, with badges that read, 'Doom Soldier' on them. They jumped off their jet-skis and straight away, every soldier turned on them.
'I've got a feeling these guys are ghosts,' Otto said in a worried tone.
Bang! Suddenly they were trapped in a huge, rusty cage which had cobwebs dangling from bar to bar, and spiders and maggots crawling in its bars. They screamed, they cried, they yelled, but the soldiers did not care. They just pushed the cage into the sea where it slowly began to sink. The children panicked and tried to break out of the cage, but it was no good, because even though the cage was covered in rust, it was as strong as a rhino.

Suddenly, a ghostly white hand appeared, followed by a ghostly white body, which opened the cage. The children stared and slowly, they also began to turn into the same ghostly white colour and they slowly began to be able to breathe again. They tried to talk and they could. They had become the ghosts of Doom Island.

Rizwan Asghar (11)
Farsley Farfield Primary School

SPOOKY LAND

One day, Mel went to Alex's house to practise some cheers for their school, Recho Carni High. Alex went downstairs to get some drinks. Mel wanted a towel to wipe off her sweat. Mel knew where they were kept, so she went to the linen closet, where she saw a black hole. Mel put her hand in the hole and something started to suck her. She was sucked right in. A flash of lightning went, and she found herself in front of a man. Now she knew Alex was a witch. The man started to say, 'Welcome to Spooky Land. Ha, ha, ha, ha. Sorry, the king makes me do that. You must go and see the king. Are you a witch?'
'No, a mortal,' said Mel.
'You'd better watch out, the king does not like mortals.'
'I'll just say I want to become immortal.'
'OK.'
So they went to the castle in the centre of Spooky Land.

The man and Mel went into the castle where the king was sucking the blood out of a mortal.
'Lauren! (That's his wife) Get me some more mortals!'
'Mark, Lauren, this is a mortal who would like to become immortal.'
'Bring her in.'
'OK Boss, here she is.'
'Let's do the test of mortal or witch.'
Suddenly, Alex burst in.
'She is a mortal,' cried the king.
Alex pushed the king back. The queen did the wrong spell and Mel became immortal. Mel ran out of the gate, through the door and back to Alex's house. Alex came soon after.
Mel said, 'I'm never coming to your house again,' and they started laughing.

Emma Williamson (8)
Farsley Farfield Primary School

THE EYE OF HELL

I awoke, scared and shaken from my nightmare. I had had a nightmare about the eye of Hell. This is a room with a triangle in the middle. You give your blood to open it.

There was only one girl to ever open it, she was called Emerald. She had black hair, black eyes and blue and red veins popping out of her face. Her mother was a witch and her dad was a goblin, so were her brothers. It was a hard life, until one day, she found the eye of Hell! Her mum and dad started treating her really badly, so she disappeared.

100 years later, a little girl called Ruby opened the triangle and sucked the life out of Emerald. She haunts the eye of Hell to this very day.

Melissa Porter (9)
Farsley Farfield Primary School

THE SPOOKY HOUSE

There was a man who lived in a spooky house. Every night before he went to sleep, he heard a noise. It went *woooo, bump, bang, aahhh!* Sometimes he thought someone was spying on him and it was a bit mad. So one night, he heard something coming down the steps. His door opened wide. *Argh!* The man fell down on the floor covered in blood!

Five years later, a woman called Emily and her two kids moved in. One day, they all went to the shop. When they came back, the house had fallen to bits. There was a note for Emily. She opened the note and fell down. The children fell and cracked their heads and that was the end of that old house.

The ghost went to another old house. What is going to happen to the next person in that house?

Jessica Sims-Walton (9)
Farsley Farfield Primary School

CHOCOLATE LAND

Chocolate Land, as you know, is made out of chocolate. In the middle of Chocolate Land there is the chocolate mansion of the Prime Minister Chocolate. In his mansion, he had chocolate windows, well, chocolate everything.

He had three chocolate slaves and a chocolate wife. Every time he was hungry, he would just go over to the sofa and chew it. He loved caramel sofas, even if they made his teeth rotten. He didn't care.

One day, Chocolate asked his chocolate wife if she could buy a new sofa because Chocky, their dog, and Chocolate had both eaten it. Later on through the day, Chocolate got home early so he didn't lose his voice telling all his slaves to get working, but it was no use. When he opened the door, he saw a new sofa. Then he saw his wife laying on the floor, half eaten by Chocky. Chocolate took her to the chocolate factory to fit more chunks of chocolate in. When she was whole again, they all walked home happily, without Chocky. Chocky was getting made into Maltesers.

Emily Webster (9)
Farsley Farfield Primary School

SPOOKY LAND

Enter the golden gates of Spooky Land if you dare . . . because the horror is waiting inside! Bloodthirsty barbarians invade every house and destroy every human! Screams of terror echo in this dark, sinister world. The only surviving animal is the fire-breathing dragon that has ruled the land for centuries. Bones break as the children of terror crunch your bones. Messages are written in blood on the walls, such as, 'Beware of the flesh-eating bull!'

One day, a girl named Shirley heard about Spooky Land. She didn't know of the terror inside and she knew some day she would dare to enter the gates and she would take over Spooky Land. Now Shirley always got her own way, and if she didn't, she would scream.

It was a Wednesday morning and Shirley had asked her mum if she could go to Spooky Land. She lied and said it was an amusement park! So her parents said yes (Shirley could go anywhere as long as she had permission). So Shirley went to Spooky Land.

When she opened the gate, a cold shiver trickled down her spine. She took one step forward and then another. *Crunch.* 'Argh!' screamed Shirley. Suddenly she felt hot breath on her back. She turned around and saw a great big, fire-breathing dragon.

'Excuse me,' said Shirley, 'will you take me to the leader?'
'I am the leader,' replied the dragon.
'I want to take over this land, will you let me?'
'No,' said the dragon, 'we rule this world and always will do!'
'Argh!' screamed Shirley, as the dragon ate her up in one gulp!

And she was never seen again.

Lauren Guest (8)
Farsley Farfield Primary School

ALIEN

Once, far out in the galaxy, there was a ship that was invaded by a horrible monster. It was invaded ten years ago and had never come back. This is the story of *The Guno*...

1991. I was watching my mum set off on a rocket, when this big animal zoomed through the sky, then I knew something was wrong. The ship set off for a horrible journey. The ship was not under control, it zoomed into hyper-space until they could not see Earth.

Then a few days later, a horrible, horrible surprise awaited them. An alien called The Guno attacked. It had been born out of its mother's mouth and had destroyed every planet in its way. It dug into the ship and ate one passenger! Soon the alien had dug into the electrical system, then 'Argh', it had eaten the second passenger, and after seeing the second die, it went for the last. It made its way and jumped, but missed. My mum then came and killed the monster. We came back to Earth and then fixed the ship!

William Buck (8)
Farsley Farfield Primary School

BECKY'S BAD DREAM

There once lived a happy little girl called Becky, who dreamed of seeing a ghost. People asked why, but all Becky replied was, 'I don't know.'

One day when Becky was walking home, everything seemed different. The street was full of fire. Becky couldn't understand. When she went home, she found her mum was a witch with a wart on the end of her long, pointed nose. Then in stepped her dad with his arms straight out and his red eyes gleaming straight at her. She screamed and ran out of the room, into the garden. In the garden, there was slime as grass and bones as a path. The bushes were on fire, the wind was blowing wildly. Everyone was going crazy!

Suddenly, *bang, bang!* Becky had had a very bad dream. But had she? Nobody knows except for Becky, but Becky will never, never tell.

Rebecca Brown (8)
Farsley Farfield Primary School

THE RAINDROP

One gloomy day, one sad raindrop was just about to fall from the sky when, just then, a big giant opened his huge mouth and gulp, slurp, swallow! The raindrop looked round the enormous mouth and slowly dropped down to the back of the mouth of the massive giant and slipped and slid down the throat with some other raindrops that had fallen into the trap with him.

Then a big rumble sounded, like thunder. Suddenly the belly started to tip and turn and then Natale, the raindrop next to him, started to get scared and - *splat* - the raindrops were out. But then they thought for a minute or two. They were in a small kind of shape. They were in the toilet. Then the giant flushed the toilet and they were sucked down into the sewers of Hell. The small raindrop of laughter was gone forever.

Rachel Smith (9)
Farsley Farfield Primary School

THE SCARY HOUSE

'Aahhh.' There was something in his cupboard. 'Help, Mum!'
'Shall I have a look?' Mum looked in and said, 'There's nothing there.'
'Help!' Now there was something under his pillow. 'Have a look here, too!'
'There is nothing there either,' said Mum.
'Mum, it must be a ghost.'
'There's no such things as ghosts, love.'
'Ooowww!'
'What was that?'
'It was the ghost, Mum.'
'Oh you know there is are no such things as ghost.'
They were both very scared by now. They were the only ones in the house and they didn't know where the ghost was, so they began to move all over.

The very nice lady next door could now hear all the noise and so came round to see if they were both all right. When she knocked, the door flew straight open. She went upstairs and the floorboards moved. By now, she wanted to go back to her house, but she wanted to check all was fine. Upstairs, there were Jill and Pete, her kids, shouting, 'Are you all right?'

They could hear the floorboards moving, but she never answered back. They went near and there was nothing. The old lady never came back.

Lucy Cross (9)
Farsley Farfield Primary School

THE MAGIC TUNNEL

One morning when Katie woke up, she got dressed and went to visit her friends, Natalie and Kerry. 'Bye Mum, bye Dad, bye Ashley,' said Katie.

Katie called for Kerry and they both went to Natalie's.
'We are looking forward to camping in the garden,' said Natalie.
'No, we are camping in the deep, dark forest,' said Katie.

The girls all helped to carry the tent there. When they had put the tent in the wood, they went straight to sleep, but Kerry heard something rustling in the trees. She went outside to see what it was. There was a light and a scary noise above her. Then it went away, but left a magic tunnel. Kerry thought she was seeing things. She went inside the tent to get the girls, but they didn't believe her, so she went down the hole herself. She could walk through walls, it was amazing. Then she saw something gold, so she went over to it. 'Wow, real gold,' said Kerry. She took a bucket and got some gold, then she went back to the tent and told the girls that they were rich! They all celebrated.

Charlotte Wakefield (9)
Farsley Farfield Primary School

A Day In The Life Of Mistary Magit

Hello there, my name is Mistary Magit. I am a silky, short magit with a silver body and golden spots. I live in a small hole with my mum and dad. I enjoy making funny faces in the warm, moist soil.

I would like to tell you what happened to me last Thursday. I was crawling along like a normal magit, when suddenly I tripped up and fell into a rock. A pitch-black crow pecked at the rock and *crack!* I thought I saw light. I was free again! I crawled back inside my warm house. I learnt I should not go out on my own. I went to sleep in my warm bed again.

Joe Howard (9)
Farsley Farfield Primary School

A Day In The Life Of Sophie Snail

Hello there! My name is Sophie Snail. I have a small brown shell and big eyes.

It started like any ordinary day. I woke up, had my breakfast, brushed my teeth and got dressed. It was a rainy day, I went outside in the back garden and went behind lots of bushes, but I got lost and didn't know what to do. Then I had an idea. I could follow my slime, so that is what I did. I followed my slime and found my way back home. I got to a big rock next to my house, climbed on it, then I fell off. I was lucky I did not smash my shell. Then I went inside my house.

Bethany Sommerville (8)
Farsley Farfield Primary School

A Day In The Life Of William Worm

Hello there, my name is William Worm. I am the longest, cleverest worm in the world. I have zigzags on me. I am pink, red and orange. I live underground with my mum and dad.

I would like to tell you about what happened to me last Friday. I was sitting in my garden when I saw my friends playing. Just the, I was playing on my mini computer when Tracy came and said to me, 'Do you want to play hide-and-seek?'
I went silent for a minute, then I said, 'Who is playing?'
Tracy said, 'Me, Adam and Mr Bird.'
I thought for a bit, then said to myself, 'I can trick Mr Bird by going underground. He's so thick he won't know what's hit him.' Then I said to Tracy, 'OK then.'

So I went over to Tracy, Adam and dumb Mr Bird. The dumb Mr Bird said, 'I want to be it.'
So I went over to a tree and hid behind it. Then Mr Bird saw me, so I wiggled underground. Mr Bird, on the other hand, looked for me for ages. After a while, he gave up and went home crying and sulking.

Amy Slater (8)
Farsley Farfield Primary School

A Day In The Life Of Larry Ladybird

Hello there, my name is Larry Ladybird. I'm probably the smallest ladybird in the world. I am as red as a tomato and have five black dots on my back.

I would like to tell you about what happened last Monday. I was in my trash bin that had been filled with bags, when a big truck turned up and poured me and my family in. I always hated being small, but now it was time to put it into action. I climbed out of a small hole while my family was crushed. I'm glad I'm small and I'm definitely moving trash bins.

Jordan Cummings (8)
Farsley Farfield Primary School

A Day In The Life Of Slithery Snail

Hello, my name is Slithery Snail. I have a brown and black shell. My actual body is brown. I live in a hole with my mum and dad. Let me tell you about last Monday.

I was playing hide-and-seek with my friends. They found me straight away because they followed my trail, so it was easy for them to find me, until one day I got an excellent idea.

I got up really early and walked all over the garden and found a long maze. Later, me and my friends got up and played hide-and-seek, but they took ages to find me because they followed my trail and it took an hour to find me. I have learnt that leaving a trail can be good fun!

Hollie Kent (8)
Farsley Farfield Primary School

A Day In The Life Of Sally Snail

Hello, my name is Sally Snail. I am very slow. I have leading trails which lead to where I live, and eyes coming out of my head. I am one of the slowest animals in the world. I live on leaves and my favourite part is the stalk I sleep on.

I am one of the youngest snails on Snail Land. I have got half a shell and the others have a full one. They always make fun of me, which makes me upset. I try to ignore them, but I can't. I've tried to grow the other half, but it still won't grow. I need a new shell for snail races, gliding and climbing. We have many races, but I always come last. The others say if you have a full shell, you become faster and win.

Megan Ingram (8)
Farsley Farfield Primary School

A Day In The Life Of Kie Caterpillar

Hello, my name is Kie, I'm a caterpillar. I'm green, quite thin and when it's damp, I shine in the light. I have hundreds of legs, but no arms. I live in the most magnificent garden. The leaves are juicy and the lush green grass is delicious.

I would like to tell you about last Monday. It started as a normal Monday. I woke up, ate breakfast, then started to climb higher up the tree in which I love, when an enormous bird swooped down to get me. I started to climb down the tree. The bird knocked me down and I fell and fell, further and further down in the air. I landed in the lush green grass, which camouflaged me, since I'm green. I crawled back home.

I have now learnt not to climb so high up the tree. I will see you when I get out of my cocoon.

Corri Stevenson (9)
Farsley Farfield Primary School

A DAY IN THE LIFE OF SARAH SNAIL

Hello there, my name is Sarah Snail. I live under a green, leafy bush. Me and my family move all around different gardens and we always find somewhere to live.

I would like to tell you what happened last Wednesday.

I was telling my family that I wanted my shell to be like everyone else's, but they just did not listen. So, as usual, I went into some gardens and one of the gardens had a pot of bright pink paint on the doorstep. Then I climbed to the top of the paint and it was very slippery. When I reached the rim, I slipped in. When I came back out, my shell was covered in pink Barbie paint. So I leapt off the rim and rushed back through the gardens to my mum and dad's house.
They said, 'You are like all of us now.'
And so I felt really happy for the first time in my life.

Holly Smith (8)
Farsley Farfield Primary School

A Day In the Life Of Carl Caterpillar

Hello there, my name is Carl. I am a caterpillar. I think I am one of the smallest bugs in the world! My bright green body has hundreds of tiny sections.

I would like to tell you what happened to me last Wednesday. I went outside to play and I fell into some mud and a bird thought I was a worm. The bird chased me around the garden five times in an hour. That got the mud off me, but that silly bird was still after me, so I camouflaged myself in the grass and from then on, I was careful not to fall into the mud again.

Liam Hemingway (9)
Farsley Farfield Primary School

A Day In the Life Of Carlos The Caterpillar

Hello, my name is Carlos the Caterpillar. I am light green, like the colour of leaves in the forest. I have really sharp teeth, so I can bite the leaves. I am a very fast runner. I live in a tree, a very sweet tree.

I would like to tell you about what happened last Monday. When I was on the way to my friend's house, I suddenly found out I couldn't move. Then I saw a bird circling above me. I remembered I was green, so I camouflaged myself. When the bird had gone, I ate the leaf and went home.

I'll never go on a sticky leaf again!

Nathanael Brown (9)
Farsley Farfield Primary School

A Day In The Life Of Sophie Butterfly

Hello, my name is Sophie Butterfly. I am pink with purple spots. I am quite small, apart from my wings. They are lilac with creamy spots and I fly quite fast. I live in a flower bed with my mum, my dad and my little brother and sister.

I would like to tell you what happened last Monday. When I went out of the garden, I flittered away to the sky and all of a sudden, I saw a black cat. I started to go down to the ground, but then the cat started to chase me. When it was about to catch me, I flew into a flower that was the same colour as me. The cat turned around, then I flittered away to the sky and landed at home, and then because the cat couldn't find me, he gave up.

Alexandra Fawcett (9)
Farsley Farfield Primary School

A Day In The Life Of A Wiggly Worm

Hello, my name is Wiggly Wiggly Worm. I am as small as your finger. I'm pink and bouncy. I have five hearts. When I'm dirty, I sparkle like glitter. I would like to tell you a story.

Last Thursday, I was wriggling along trying to find my lunch, when suddenly it got dark and I was nearly cut in two by a lawnmower. I quickly bounced on it and slowly went round the garden. I saw the thing that people live in. I kept stopping because the lawnmower was broken. Then it started again. When I got off, I thought it was like Alton Towers theme park.

David Burrell (8)
Farsley Farfield Primary School

A Day In The Life Of Lucy Ladybird

Hello, my name is Lucy Ladybird. I am bright red with hundreds of black spots all over my back.

I would like to tell you what happened to me last Friday. I was in a field quite happily looking for some food, when a huge brown bird spotted me and carried me off to her nest. She dropped me into her nest full of baby sparrows.
One of the sparrows said, 'You are beautiful, we couldn't eat you.' So she flipped me out of the nest and I spread my beautiful wings and flew off into the field.

Lauren Hanson (7)
Farsley Farfield Primary School

A Day In The Life Of Clio Caterpillar

Hello there, my name is Clio Caterpillar. I have yellow spots along my body.

I would like to tell you about what happened to me last Monday. I went into my back garden and a huge black cat grabbed me and started throwing me around. Then the cat dropped me down a fox hole and I landed on the fox's head. Then suddenly, I turned into a butterfly and flew out of the hole, over the cat and as it jumped to catch me it missed. I flew too high for it!

Ashley Nicholson (9)
Farsley Farfield Primary School

A Day In The Life Of Chloe Caterpillar

Hello there, my name is Chloe. I am just like any caterpillar. I live on a piece of cardboard. I do not look pretty, but I look normal. Soon I will turn into a cocoon and I feel really worried that I may stay like this forever.

But then one glorious, sunny day, I will come out of my cocoon and I will be a beautiful butterfly. I will never be sad about my looks again.

Charlotte Beattie (8)
Farsley Farfield Primary School

A Day In The Life Of Cordell Caterpillar

Hello, my name is Cordell Caterpillar. I am a long caterpillar with red and blue spots on me. Everybody says I am really beautiful. I am the fastest caterpillar in the world! Do you want to hear what happened to me last Friday?

It started off as a normal day. I had my breakfast, then I went off down to the bottom of the garden. I have never been at the bottom of the garden before. I was wriggling along the grass, when suddenly I saw two shadows. One was big and one was small. I looked up and there was an enormous tree and an enormous blackbird above me. I was terrified. I said to myself, 'How can that bird see me? My blue and red spots!' It was then I realised it wasn't very good to be beautiful anymore.

There was mud beneath me. I quickly covered myself in mud so the blackbird couldn't see me. In about a minute, the bird flew away. When I got home my mum said, 'Go in the bath now.' I just laughed.

Jessica Louise Nunn (8)
Farsley Farfield Primary School

A Day In The Life Of Fussy Fly

Hello, my name is Fussy Fly. I am yellow and black. I have a little spike at the end of me.

I would like to tell you what happened to me last Tuesday.

Well, it started off like any normal Tuesday. My mum and my dad made my breakfast and I went outside. My neighbours asked my mum if I was playing out. My mum told them I was round the back. When they came round, they found I was stuck in a spiderweb.
My neighbours saw me in the web and they said, 'Stop messing about, let's go and see the workers.'
The others went to see them, but I shouted, 'What about me?'
They said, 'Oh yes, what about Fussy? Come on, let's help him out of that sticky stuff. Go on guys, we'll meet you there.'

Soon I was free and that taught me not to play on my own and off we went.

Jacob Bowers (8)
Farsley Farfield Primary School

A Day In The Life Of Henry Centipede

Hello, my name is Henry Centipede. I am quite long and I have lots of legs. I live with my mum and dad at the bottom of the garden, under a stone. I would like to tell you what happened last Tuesday.

I was out for a walk when I was passing this sign, it said, *Come To The Insect Run On 11th June.* So I went home and got my shoes and started to exercise. The race started at 1pm the next afternoon. I was so excited, I forgot to tie my shoelaces.

The race started and we all started to run. It was a little bit like a marathon. I started to feel the path on my feet and realised I had lost my shoes. Then we came to the finish line and I came second.

After the race, I went back to where I had been running and there I found my shoes, but they all had holes in them!

Samantha Stringer (8)
Farsley Farfield Primary School

A Day In The Life Of Weird Worm

Hello, my name is Weird Worm. I am a little brown, wriggly thing just like a party sausage. I would like to tell you what happened to me last Sunday.

I fell out with my mum over her taking my phone off me, so I ran away into the cool, dark night and settled down near a lake. Next morning, I woke up and found myself flying. I thought it was unusual, but who cares? Then I found out I was not flying, I was fishing. 'OK, don't panic. I'm about to be killed,' I said to myself.

The spike on the hook was so sharp I held my breath, waiting to be killed.
'Tea time, Tom,' the man said.
'OK,' replied Tom.
Tom dropped me. 'Yes!' I said. I decided to go straight home, but I slid into a lamp post and nearly went down a drain. 'Oh dear, this isn't going very well, is it?' I said.

Soon, I got home and made friends with my mum again.

Timothy Corcoran (8)
Farsley Farfield Primary School

A Day In The Life Of Sammy Snail

Hello, my name is Sammy Snail. I think I am one of the stickiest snails in the world! I may be fat, but I have a big heart. I've got a golden-silver shell that protects me from danger.

I would like to tell you what happened to me last Wednesday. It all began as a normal day. My mum made me breakfast and then I went out. I went to the part of the garden where there was a huge rock. I climbed the rock and I could feel the soft breeze of summer. All of a sudden, I was stuck on the huge rock. I screamed, 'Oh no! A person is gong to stand on me!' Well, I was lucky, the person just missed me. Look, there's a bird looking for food.

While I was on the rock, I found out I was safe at least for now. Well it is not too bad being the stickiest. That is what happened to me on Wednesday.

Roberta Hall (8)
Farsley Farfield Primary School

A Day In The Life Of Lisa Ladybird

Hello, my name is Lisa Ladybird. I am very small. I am red, white and black. I have six small white spots on my wings and I live in a big crack in the floor.

It all started on Monday when my sisters began to pick on me because I was small, but luckily Mum loves me more. So that day, I went with my sisters on an adventure. We found a field and it was covered in strange objects. We didn't realise that it was a rubbish dump. Then the wind started to blow, so we went to investigate the objects. We found a rusty old chest. We all flew inside, when suddenly a huge gust of wind slammed the chest lid shut. We all started to panic and we cried for help. I found a small hole that I aimed through, but my plump sisters couldn't get out, so I went for help from my insect friends. Within an hour, over a thousand of my insect friends of different shapes and sizes arrived at the dump.

My sisters now know that being small isn't bad after all, and they now know why Mum loves me more.

Rebecca Laurie (8)
Farsley Farfield Primary School

A Day In The Life Of Simon Centipede

One day, Simon went for a walk. He kept on getting his legs tangled up with the grass. When he tried to pick up a leg, he picked up the grass, and when he tried to pick up grass, he picked up a leg. It was all because he was green.

The next day, he saw some red paint, then had an idea. He went to dip his legs in, then he let them dry. When they had dried, he went for a walk again and never worried ever again.

Chloe Waite (8)
Farsley Farfield Primary School

A Day In The Life Of A Rabbit

I am brown and furry and I have red eyes. I live in a rabbit hole in the ground. People are always putting their hands down it.

One day, it was play time for the children and they began stepping on my home. I hopped out of my rabbit hole and scared them all away. They never came back to my home again and I lived happily ever after.

Michaela Nutter (8)
Farsley Farfield Primary School

THE HAUNTED HOTEL

One night, a grandma and her granddaughter went to a hotel in Blackpool. They didn't know it was haunted. They went to the reception and asked for a key for a room. He turned round and whispered, 'Do you know what you are doing?'

They went upstairs to their room. The girl got changed while her grandma was in the shower. The girl then heard a noise, turned around, but couldn't see anything. She went in the bathroom and told her grandma she had heard a noise. Her grandma didn't reply, so the girl pulled back the shower curtain and saw her grandma hung up on the wall, dead. There was no water coming out of the shower head, just blood. The girl was frightened, she couldn't do anything else but just go to bed.

Suddenly, when lying in her bed, she heard a tap on the window. She turned round, but could only see a blood mark where the person had been. She hid under her covers, then heard someone come in. She closed her eyes saying to herself, 'It's just a dream.'

It was soon morning. Her grandma was fine, but there was a message in blood on the wall saying, 'I'll get you next time.'

Jessica Townsley (10)
Farsley Farfield Primary School

THE NEW BOY ON THE BLOCK

Once upon a time there was a boy called Sammy who came to live in a town called Bolton Moor. This town was only a short distance from the main ring road and was often used by travellers or gypsies as a stopping off point for them.

One day, Sammy was walking his dog called Scott near to where the gypsy caravans were and he saw some children playing. He stopped to watch them and when they asked him if he would like to join them in a game of football, he was very pleased. He wanted to know where he could leave his dog so it wouldn't be in the way of the ball game. They told him to leave the dog tied up near to where they were playing, but out of the way of the ball so it wouldn't get hurt. This he did and then the game of football (five-a-side) began.

Sammy immediately went into the attack and aimed for goal, doing a brilliant left-footed shot straight into the top right hand corner of the goal. A great cheer went up for the new boy in the team. Sammy felt very pleased with himself as he didn't get to play with many children and he loved football. He was always watching it on TV. They started to kick-off again, but there were no more goals scored, although Sammy tried really hard to score another goal for his team. The match ended 1-0.

When the match was over, Sammy went to get Scott because it was time to go home for tea, and his mum would be waiting for him.

Benjamin Matthews (10)
Farsley Farfield Primary School

THE HAUNTED HOUSE

I was just about to eat my brain soup when there was a knock on the door, so I held my knife in my left hand, tightly. Then I looked through he keyhole and there was nobody there, so I turned around. The floorboards were creaking and the tables were moving. I stopped for two seconds and then ran upstairs and locked myself in my bedroom and waited.

After ten minutes, I could hear the stairs moving, like someone was walking on them, so I went out and I saw a moving, invisible person walking towards me. I ran inside my bedroom and locked my door, then I went to get my knife. The door started to bang, so I hid under my bed. My hands were shaking and the door was opening. I couldn't see anybody coming through the door, so I gradually made my way out from under the bed. I stood up and nobody was there, so I peeped outside my door and I went downstairs. I had my blade up just in case anything came up to me. I went to lock the door and then I went to phone a friend to come to the house and keep me company.

My friend came over and knocked on the door. I went to unlock the door so she could come in.
She said to me, 'Are you alright?'
'I'm alright!' I said.

Adam Wild (10)
Farsley Farfield Primary School

The Jewellery Theft

It was midnight in London. A shady character was moving slowly up Westminster Road. The mystery person was wearing a long, black robe that went from his head to his toes. He had a hood over his face. The strange person was nearly at the top of the road. He put one of his steel-like hands into his pocket and pulled out a glass-cutter. He finally reached the jewellery store and cut a hole in the glass. He climbed in and took the Royal Arabian jewels and then disappeared.

Police sirens echoed around Westminster Road. The police were looking for clues to who was the thief. There were no signs of any finger marks.
'This thief must be very sly,' said Chief John. 'There are no footprints leading out of the store,' said John. John decided to call for Karl Johnson, a world famous detective.

Two days after the robbery, Karl arrived at the police headquarters with his assistant, James.
'Ah, at last you're here,' said John.
'I hear that the Arabian jewels have been stolen,' said Karl.
'That's right,' said John.
'Have you found any clues?' asked James.
'No,' said John.
'We should go to the place where the crime was committed,' said Karl.
James shivered with fear.

Karl, James and John went to the jewellery store with a police force. James had sneakily taken a sniper with him.
'Mmm,' said Karl, 'this mystery is becoming beyond my capabilities.'

'Maybe there are some clues upstairs,' suggested James, 'I'll go have a look.' He went upstairs and opened a window. Karl had gone outside. James aimed the sniper at Karl, he fired and Karl fell, almost dead.
'I've worked out who the thi . . . ef is,' he stuttered, 'it is . . .' Karl was dead.

The theft of the jewels remained unsolved.

Connor Robinson (10)
Farsley Farfield Primary School

THE NIGHTMARE VISIT

Megan and Matthew were bored. It was late Saturday afternoon and they couldn't decide what to do. They were staring out of the window and kept glancing at an old abandoned house over the road.

Megan looked at Matthew and spoke, 'That house looks spooky, would you dare to go in there when it's dark?'

Suddenly, Matthew's eyes opened wide and a big cheesy smile spread across his face. 'We could go tonight while Mum is watching that yucky romantic film, that one she's been wittering on about,' said Matthew excitedly.

They both ran eagerly down the stairs and asked their mum if they could play out.

It was getting quite dark as Matthew and Megan were putting their coats and shoes on. For the first time, Matthew was feeling nervous. They left the house.

'Here we are, the house of doom. Come on,' joked Megan, though she was also scared a ghost or monster might hear them and come out on them.

They had just stepped into the first room when the moonlight shone through the window and they saw the shadow of a body with a head hanging off. They stood there shaking as much as you would when you get electrocuted, until they screamed a very faint scream, and both said at the same time, 'Get . . . us . . . out . . . of . . . here!'

They turned and ran into an old dummy whose head was hanging off!

They kept running, tripped over a few twigs and when they got home, they slammed the door shut.

'Never again!' they both shouted.

Lucy Maude (10)
Farsley Farfield Primary School

THE GHOST ON HALLOWE'EN

One Hallowe'en night when it was thundering and lightning, a little boy called Josh, who had just turned fourteen and his little sister Sophie, who was ten, were out trick or treating around the block near where they lived.
Josh said to his little sister, 'Why don't we be heading for home now?'
Then a quiet voice appeared from nowhere, 'No, you must not go yet. The fun hasn't begun.'
Sophie whispered to her older brother, 'Can we go? I'm scared. Please, Josh?'
The voice replied, 'There's no need to be scared. You're fine with me.'
Josh thought in his mind for a bit and said to Sophie, 'Look at my fingers and when I show three, we will run back home and we will then be safe.'
Sophie cried to Josh, 'I'm so sorry this has happened tonight. It's all my fault. How can I repay you?'
'Don't worry, you didn't know that something terrible was going to happen like this, did you?'
'No, I suppose so. Josh, Mum and Dad might be back. They will probably be wondering where we are.'

The ghost had lost track of where they had wandered off to. He was then talking to himself. 'When I see more kids, I am going to bash their heads and make my own sandwiches.'

The ghost from that night was going around searching street to street until he found a little boy. Shocked, the boy turned around and said, 'Who is that?' Then very strongly, 'You do not need to dress up and pretend, because I know it's a costume!'

Amy Stevenson (9)
Farsley Farfield Primary School

MY HOSPITAL STAY

It started when I was five years old. We were out shopping, Mum was getting me a new coat, when I started to get stomach pains.

The next day, we went to my granma Mo's for tea. She said I looked poorly. I didn't eat much tea as the pains were getting worse.

The next day I stayed off school. On the Wednesday morning, Mum was helping me get dressed. I told her that my tummy still hurt. Mum took me to the doctor, who pressed my tummy. It hurt a lot. She said I had to go to the hospital. She thought it was appendicitis.

I went up for a scan. They put cold gel on my tummy and on a TV screen, they could see inside me. I would need an operation that night. I could not eat or drink until after the operation. The nurse came and put cream on my hand. Dad came.

I went down to the operating theatre, Mum stayed with me. They put a needle in my hand (where the cream was. I don't know, I couldn't feel it.) The next thing I remember was Dad saying, 'It's all over, Amy.'

I had to stay in the hospital for seven days because my temperature was high and I had an infection. I was on a drip.

I was off school for two weeks. I will always have a scar, but so does my granma and for the same reason.

Amy Mitchell (9)
Farsley Farfield Primary School

AMERICAN MISFIT

'Snob.'
'Geek.'
'Fatso.' Is all I hear every morning as I'm walking to school.

Hi, my name's Lucy. Hannah and Claire are the worst people on Earth! They have been bullying me all through semester because they have just joined my school, Manhattan High. I don't know what to do. If I try telling a teacher, they threaten to beat me up. *Help!* I'm going to write a diary of all the things they do to me, so here it is.

7th October, 2002

Today was horrible, I had a maths test where I had to give all the answers to Hannah, or she would kill me. Also, I have just finished Claire's history homework. I have decided I really need to tell somebody. If I don't, who knows what will happen to me? How about a letter to Mrs Patrick about them - would they find out?

10th October, 2002

Today Mrs Patrick gave Claire's homework full marks, then said that I had copied her! As I was walking to maths, Hannah purposely tripped me up and started laughing. I have now broken my foot. I told my mum that I fell in the yard - what else could I say? Everybody in Year 8 knows about them bullying me, but won't say anything. Today Melissa Brown saw Hannah trip me up, but didn't do anything. I have really thought about it and I have decided to show Mrs Patrick my dairy. Every day I stare at the problem box, thinking my letter should be in there and it finally is!

Jasmine Cheema (10)
Farsley Farfield Primary School

Gone

It was a sunny day in Leeds and I was moving into a new house. I was moving from Liverpool, so it would be a change for me. We hadn't looked at the house, but it was big enough. When I walked into the house, it was bigger than it looked. I ran upstairs to find the biggest bedroom, which of course is now mine. It was just the right size for me. The bedroom was decorated with flowers. It had purple walls with different flowers. It didn't look like wallpaper. I just couldn't wait to go to sleep in my new room.

It was starting to get dark and I had to go to bed. My dad had moved my bed earlier. I was ready for bed and it was only 8.30pm I got into bed and was nearly asleep when I heard a noise. It sounded like it was coming from the bathroom, so I went to check it out. There wasn't anybody there, but I still heard a voice. It was saying, 'I am a ghost and I will get you.'
'Arrghhh!' I screamed as I ran downstairs. *'Help!'* I shouted. 'There is a ghost upstairs and it's gonna get me.'
'Don't be stupid, Holly,' they said.
I got back into bed and they gave me a kiss.

The next morning, police were all round the house and Holly's mum and dad were talking to them.
'We woke up this morning to find that she was *gone!*'

Jessica Williamson (10)
Farsley Farfield Primary School

THE BIRTHDAY RIDE

Yesterday it was my birthday. I had a party at a theme park. My name is Millie and I'll tell you all about how I overcame my fear.

Me and my friends had just come off a slow ride and stepped into the queue for the next ride - the Corkscrew! It was a roller coaster that had an enormous drop and two scary loop-the-loops. My hands were shaking and my brain was saying, 'Don't do this, don't do this!' But I really wanted to and I couldn't walk away.

Suddenly I heard the man cry, 'Next fifteen please!' To my dismay, I realised I was one of them. I clambered into the carriage next to my best friend. I pulled down the shoulder harness and sat back and started to whimper, 'Why am I doing this? Why?' Then I rubbed my eyes and looked ahead of me. The carriage was cranking up the steep slope, then *whoosh!* We hurtled down the biggest drop of the ride, the wind in my hair as I screamed at the top of my voice. I stopped screaming as we came to the first loop-the-loop. Upside down, I was hanging onto my harness in fear of falling out. Then came the second one, we whizzed round. By that time I was laughing!

The carriage rattled to the humps, we went up and down, my bottom was in the air. Last of all, the carriage chugged to a stop. I had overcome my fear and mastered the Corkscrew and I had done it on my special birthday. I had learned that if you don't try things, you'll never know if you like them!

Emily Killoran (10)
Farsley Farfield Primary School

A Day In The Life Of A Frog

I am a frog. I have four legs and all the giants pick me up and chuck me around.

One day, while playing, I went flying into the pond. I landed next to my friends. I got back out, jumped and went back to see my other friends. Then me and my friends played hide-and-seek. I was the last one to be found. We played another game before we all went home to bed in our pond.

Jordan Anderson (7)
Farsley Farfield Primary School

A Day In The Life Of A Spider

I am a spider. I look like a hairy freak. I have eight legs to walk on and I can also make a web. I live in the playground.

One day I was having dinner when just at that moment, I heard a noise. I had a look and I saw all the children rushing and barging, coming out to play. I had just got out of the way before they opened the door. I nearly died, but I managed to get away. One of them picked me up and I bit him. He went off crying and then came back. They then caught me in a jar, but they looked after me.

Jack Henderson (8)
Farsley Farfield Primary School

A Day In The Life Of A Caterpillar

One sunny day, a caterpillar, called Ashmiat, was sitting on a leaf when suddenly, a giant picked her up and threw her away. She later found her friends and told them what had happened. They said, 'You need to change into a butterfly.'

The next day it was raining. She found a nice dry place. She was in the apple sculpture. She wasn't in there for long, when she was scooped into a jar. The children put her in their classroom. After four weeks, they let her go free. She fell asleep.

The next day, no children touched her. She ate an apple and a crisp, then fell asleep. She changed into a butterfly and flew into the open sky.

Cordell Sutton (8)
Farsley Farfield Primary School

JULIE'S SPECIAL PRESENT

One bright morning, Julie looked around her bedroom. It was plastered with pictures of dogs that Julie liked. 'What a lovely day,' said Julie. She glanced at her calendar, it was the 18th of July. 'My birthday!' she shouted and ran downstairs to the living room, where her parents, Sally and Richard Green, were waiting for her.
'We thought that you weren't coming,' said her father joyfully.
'Where are my presents?' Julie asked.
'You'll have to find them,' answered her mother, giving her a map.
'Will you help me?' questioned Julie.
'No,' her mother said, 'but Sarah and Owen will.'
Sarah and Owen looked at the map.
'We're pirates,' said Sarah.
'I'm your special seadog and we're looking for buried treasure,' added Julie.
'This way,' said Owen, proudly holding the map.

They went to the shed, then the hedge, to the flower bed and finally up to the kitchen, where a pile of presents stood waiting.
'Open this one first, darling,' said Julie's mother.
Julie carefully opened the box and inside stood a little golden puppy, the one she had always wanted.
'I hope you like it,' her father said.
'I don't just like it, I love it!' laughed Julie happily.
'I hope you like our present,' called Sarah, giving Julie her present.
Julie tore it open. Inside was a gold collar and lead, studded with rubies.
'Thank you and I'm going to call this puppy Ruby!' Julie called out.

Jennifer Burrell (10)
Farsley Farfield Primary School

CATERPILLAR CHASE

Hi, my name's Freddy the Caterpillar and I am going to tell you the story of my trip into outer space! So, it all started at night when I was looking out of my leaves and saw the fabulous moon. I thought of how I would like to go to the moon.

The next day, I packed my bag and set off to *the moon!* As I was wandering along, I saw a huge door. Was I at the world's end? I crawled under this door, it was sheltered and roomy. I found some steps, up I went till I stopped and saw five more huge doors. I picked one of these doors and crawled under. It was space at last. I had finally found space, but where was the moon? I searched for hours and hours (ten minutes) and found a cheese, round moon-looking thing. I jumped up and down in glee to find the moon! I wondered if I was the first caterpillar to the moon. If I was, could you imagine it? *First caterpillar to the moon!*

Then I thought about all my friends and family in Leaf Land. I then calmed down a bit. They would all be looking for me, or worried that I had been put in a jar for a pet! So I headed home.

At home, I asked my friends if they had been to the moon. None of them had, so I began to tell them about my adventure.

Fay Walker (10)
Farsley Farfield Primary School

A Day In The Life Of A Dragonfly

My name is John and I am a dragonfly. I am blue and I am 18cm long.

One day when I was flying around the pond, the children came and a boy tried to squash me. I shouted, 'Help, help,' and my friends came to help me. My best friend, the wasp, stung him and they took me home because I was in a lot of pain.

They took me to their house and made the pain go away. When I was better, I went home.

Michael Mullin (8)
Farsley Farfield Primary School

A Day In The Life Of A Spider

One day, I put my web up for some food. I heard some children coming. They reached out and picked me up and I bit them, then Liam, my friend, came and helped me to bite them. They dropped me. I fell into the pond and started to drown. A child got me out and took me home. Liam went home crying. He never forgot me ever, not in his long life.

Dale Tunnicliffe (9)
Farsley Farfield Primary School

A Day In The Life Of A Spider

I am a spider. I am fat and hairy with eight legs.

One day, I was walking up the mound when some children came up and tried to flatten me. *How disgraceful,* I thought. *I am going to try and bite them on the hand.* I did and the child cried and ran away.

Later on, I felt better.

Bilal Salim (8)
Farsley Farfield Primary School

A Day In The Life Of A Spider

I'm a spider. I eat flies. Yesterday I was making a net to catch some flies when a child broke it. Now I make my nets in private, like on a building. But one day, some people came climbing and broke my net.

Now I make my nets on a plant or a leaf, where most flies go, or an apple tree with those delicious apples on it.

Patrick Miller (8)
Farsley Farfield Primary School

MAGICAL THINGS WILL HAPPEN!

Hi, my name is Claire. Did you know I had the worst baby brother in the world? He cried all day, pooped all day and got all the attention, but that wasn't the half of it. This is my story.

My mum was in hospital having a baby. I had to stay home with my nana because I was only seven and couldn't look after myself. When my mum came home, she handed me my dirty clothes to take upstairs. I ran upstairs into my bedroom and started crying while she looked after my baby brother, Alien I called him, but Mum called him Trevor. I knew he was no Trevor when I found out what he was like the next morning.

I woke up particularly early to see what Alien was doing. I caught him up to no good. He was outside turning the grass pink and, and look at me, black and white. I decided I had had enough. I grabbed hold of him. *Ouch!* He bit me. 'Mum,' I shouted, 'he bit me!'
'I know, I saw him. Get him!'

We ran all day, but finally caught him and in a rocket, we sent him off to his own planet where I knew he belonged. We never saw him again.

Victoria James (10)
Farsley Farfield Primary School

THE GHOST OF THE DRAGOON

First thing on my 10th birthday, I rushed downstairs nearly knocking my brother senseless, and gobbled down my breakfast like there was no tomorrow. Only because I didn't know what was coming today to haunt me for eternity. I excitedly opened my presents and saw a *Beyblade!* I opened it, built it and I saw my bit-chip glow purple. I knew at once it was the bit-beast Mum told me about, and it would take revenge on a certain ten-year-old. I thought I was safe, so I went out to battle Ben, and found my Beyblade ripped up the stadium. Creepy, eh? That's not all - all the books in my bag kept turning to ash.

So, next day, I battled a guy called Kai. I called out my bit-beast and released a bit-beast. I was totally scared and ran away to my hideout for some serious thinking. I schemed up an anti-Dragoon plan. I needed to battle it and win so he'd clear off for eternity. So I went to Chinatown and battled the ghost of Dragoon. I called out my bit and fired a blow so powerfully gruesome, Dragoon was gone *forever!*

So that night, me and my chums threw a party which lasted all night and drank a toast to my bit-beast.

Alaina Benn (10)
Farsley Farfield Primary School

BACK IN TIME

One cold morning, James and Jess decided to get their new bikes out of the garage. They ran outside, grabbed their helmets and rode off down to the new shop, called 'John's'.

Bang! 'It's starting to thunder,' said James, brushing his hair away from his face. Suddenly, a flash of light struck the front wheel of their bike. James and Jess both fell to the ground.

James woke up and looked around him. He noticed they were not on their way to John's, they were on the floor surrounded by trees. But not only trees, they were surrounded by . . . *dinosaurs!*

'Jess, Jess, wake up, quick!'
Jess woke up to find herself surrounded by dinosaurs. 'James, we have been brought back in time. What shall we do?'
James and Jess walked slowly and carefully past the dinosaurs. They walked through the tall trees.
'Wait,' said Jess in a scared and frightened voice, 'we are in the feeding grounds, nobody move.' A small, light brown dinosaur circled them.
'Help!' shouted James.
'James, shush now, we're going to have to run.'

They ran over rocks, under trees and down big hills, while three dinosaurs scrambled after them. Two dinosaurs were pushing and fighting. James and Jess kept on running. It started to rain and thunder and then a flash of light crashed as it hit James' and Jess' feet. Suddenly, Jess and James found themselves back beside their bikes.

Was it a dream, or did it really happen?

Abigail Morgan (10)
Farsley Farfield Primary School

THE HAUNTED HOUSE

One day, there was a boy called Josh. After moving house, he went out to play. He came across this big house-like thing. Josh went over to the house and stared at it for a moment. Then he opened the door and he went in. Suddenly, someone touched him on the back. A witch behind him said, 'I'm going to have you for my supper.'
Josh looked around and could see a faint thing in the background. Then the witch flew out of the window. The faint thing was a ghost. He told Josh his name was Bob and Josh told him he was Josh. His mum, by this time was getting worried, so he went home.

The next day, Bob took Josh to see his mates. They were called Bill and Tim. They took him to see their mate Draco the Dracula. This guy scared Josh, but he was funny. They all went into their room and told jokes.
Draco told one, he said, 'Once, there were two crisps walking along. My dad stopped and said, 'Do you want a lift?'
They said, 'No, because we're Walkers!'

They all slept where they were, and the next morning, they played football. Bob was like Ronaldo. It was him and Draco on the same team, Josh scored behind. Bill scored one, Tim wasn't very good. Bob scored three for their team. So they won 3-2. They all had a good time, but they had to go home.

Josh's mum wasn't pleased. Josh got grounded, but then again, he had a good time.

Matthew Atter (10)
Farsley Farfield Primary School

THE SCREAM

'Quickly, or we'll miss the bus!' shouted Marik to Scott. The two boys ran, but before they knew it, the bus had gone.
'Damn!' shouted Scott in an angry voice.
'Wait, I know a short cut home, it's through the graveyard.'
'Whoa, whoa, whoa, you're not getting me to go through the graveyard,' said Scott in a worried voice.
'Got any better ideas?' replied Marik.

The boys were quite scared. They should have been back a while ago, it was getting dark because it was winter.
'Argh!' screamed Marik as he fell to the bottom of a huge hole in the ground.
'Argh! You woman, it doesn't hurt,' said Scott.

The boys somehow got out of the hole and they saw a tall figure with long black hair. He, or this thing, turned around. It opened its mouth and there were two sharp, pointy teeth. The boys screamed!

Joe Sutcliffe (10)
Farsley Farfield Primary School

A Day In The Life Of A Rabbit

One day, I came up from my hole and there was no one there, so I went back in.

I came back out later that day and some children started to chase me. I was very scared, so I went back in my hole and I saw some big hands come down. I bit one and I heard a big, massive scream. So I went right to the top of the hill and never went back again.

On the top of the hill, I ran about and dug holes, then I jumped in and out of them. I had a much better time in my new home.

Emma Shaw (9)
Farsley Farfield Primary School

A Day In The Life Of An Ant

I'm an ant. I am called Chief. I lead a fleet of ants.

My fleet rushed up to a helicopter, we were just in time to jump onto it.

We formed a ladder to climb up to the main base. We saw the pilot, I told my troops to tie him up and take control of the helicopter.

We shoved him in the back and flew to an army bunker. We climbed up the drain and made an army ant base on top of the army bunker. Mission completed.

Jordan Halton (9)
Farsley Farfield Primary School

A Day In The Life Of A Rabbit

I am a beautiful white rabbit. I live in a rabbit hole, it is wide and deep. My home is really deep. I hop around on the grass. I like eating grass.

One day I went out and there were all these people coming to my hole. I got down my hole. These boys went to my hole, I went over to the mud, then I hopped over to the boys and bit them. They cried. I then went to my friend's, but got picked up on the way by this big girl. She was wearing a cross. The girl then took me home.

Daniel Anderson (8)
Farsley Farfield Primary School

THE PINK GOO

One day there lived a girl called Melissa and she was on her way to her nanna's house. When she got there she went to the kitchen and looked in all the cupboards for something to eat. When she opened the last cupboard, she found some pink goo. She decided to pour it in the bath.

While she was watching TV, suddenly a monster bath came and sat next to her. When she saw it, she started to scream. Her nanna came out of bed from her nap. She said, 'What on earth is going on in here?'
Melissa said, 'Nothing.'
'Well be quiet,' said her nanna.
'OK,' said Melissa to her nanna.

The bath monster was still next to her, but it wasn't doing anything. Melissa saw that the monster was nice, so she decided to give it some crisps to eat. But for some reason the monster wouldn't eat the crisps, so Melissa went to find it something else.
When she came back, the monster was eating her nanna's metal walking stick. Melissa got the monster some metal things to eat for the day. When it had finished all the metal things, Melissa had to go and get some more.
When she came back the bath was back in the bathroom, so she decided to go to bed.
'Night, night,' said Melissa to her nanna.

Danielle Ramsden (9)
Field Lane Primary School

THE HOUSE ON THE HILL FILLED WITH GHOSTS

One day there were three girls and one of them was called Amy. She had brown hair and brown eyes. Tiffany had brown eyes and black hair and Victoria had blonde hair and blue eyes.
They had gone for a walk on the old, dark hill.
'Victoria, come on, we're going to the creepy witch house,' said Tiffany.
'There it is,' said Amy.

They walked in and found bats were flying everywhere. Then suddenly a ghost came floating down the long, deep, white stairs beside a vampire.
'Oh, visitors,' they said.
The vampire took them to a big room where the witches closed the door with magic. The witches then went out and the ghosts filled the room. The walls began to cave in, so the girls went out of a little green trapdoor and came out on the hill.

They all ran home and never went back from then on.

Eve Hamill Murin (9)
Field Lane Primary School

A Day In The Life Of A Castle

On a dark, stormy night, it was thundering and lightning. There were three boys playing out. James was handsome and brave. Ben was intelligent and hardworking. Joshua was thin and ugly.
James dared them to go to the castle of doom. So they did.

The castle was dark and spooky, especially on such a dark night.
Joshua said, 'I'm not doing it.'
James said, 'Be brave.'
'OK, let's go then,' Josh said.
They went into the castle of doom, where they saw a nasty ghost. They ran upstairs and saw another ghost who looked less scary. They scared the other ghost away and left the house.

With their success in the ghost house, they then went on holiday to ghost island. It was full of ghosts. There was a ghost fair which was loud and full of trucks. It was very spooky and great.
They bought a new skeleton dog that was white and six inches tall. They used it for a guard dog.
They went back to the ghost house and decorated the castle white so no one could see the ghosts. Then they played hide-and-seek.

James, Joshua and Ben never found the two ghosts they saw before because of the white paint.

Benjamin Margison (9)
Field Lane Primary School

A Day In The Life Of A Swimming Pool Disaster

Emma was sitting on the messy and clustered poolside. There was a swimming gala and it was making the swimming pool hot and sweaty. There was a rainbow colour of different swimming pool T-shirts. Scattered all over the red brick benches were towels and bags.

Emma and her friends were very excited about the races. They would be starting in 15 minutes and the time seemed to rush by.

Sixteen minutes later, Emma was slowly walking over the red, squashy mats to the poolside. She was sorted into her lane by a plump and hairy man who was very kind. She was ready to dive in with her toes over the edge. The man was just about to count to three when . . .
'Wait, there's no water in the swimming pool,' a man with a sweaty face was shouting.
He was right - the ripples of the shiny water were not there.
'Oh no!' said Emma.
They couldn't have the gala, or could they?

There was a sound outside and suddenly firemen came rushing in from all directions with hosepipes. They filled the swimming pool up with shiny, rippling water and the gala went ahead. And guess what? Emma won the biggest, shiniest cup. No one will ever leave the plug out of the pool again.

Eve Morley (9)
Field Lane Primary School

BEWARE OF DRACULA

One day about 50 years ago, Dracula was born. He grew up to be a cruel little boy. Nobody knew he was evil.
His teacher, Mrs Wiggleworm, always said, *'Dracula! You're a disgrace to mankind!'*

Dracula didn't care if he got told off. He thought school was stupid, so he didn't go back. The only problem was, he saw his teacher at the shop.
'Why were you not at school today?' asked Mrs Wiggleworm.
'Bye-bye,' said Dracula and gobbled her up! 'Tasted like chicken,' said Dracula.
He went home and told his mum.
'Good boy,' she exclaimed.

He went back outside and ate everything he could see. Then he did a massive belch and everything he had eaten came out.
His teacher said, 'Stay off school as long as you like!' and ran off.

Then Dracula went to bed and thought, *I can have everything I want*, as he started to nod off.

Victoria Noble (9)
Field Lane Primary School

THE GHOST SCHOOL

One morning I got out of bed and went to the bathroom. I washed my hands and face and cleaned my teeth. Just then I heard a loud noise coming from my wardrobe. I went into my bedroom and opened my wardrobe doors. The noise stopped, so I got dressed.
'Go to school now,' said my mum.
So I went to school.

On the way I heard a noise - a spooky noise.
'I'm scared,' I said.

When I got to school, I found blood all over the floor and everyone was hiding. Ghosts and witches surrounded me and suddenly they all pounced on me, but I managed to escape.

I heard a knock at the door. It was my mum and we both ran home and had some hot chocolate.

Stacey Thornton (8)
Field Lane Primary School

A Ghost Story

Once there was a ghost that nobody ever saw. He went out on the street and asked every boy and girl if they would be his friend, but the problem was nobody knew who was talking to them. So all of the children ignored the ghost and decided to go and play away from the baker's shop. They all went off to the park and were followed by the ghost. They got an ice cream free.

'Hello, you beast, come out wherever you are,' said the children.
'I'm out, but you can't see me cos I'm an invisible person. Just touch me. Don't push or punch, alright?'
But the ghost chucked a bucket of slimy, runny goo which fell all over the children and they couldn't get it off. One of the children picked up the bucket and threw the goo on the ghost. Now they could see the ghost. The ghost was a real person and it was their friend, Lauren.
So they all became friends again and got up to mysteries every day.

Michelle Holland (9)
Field Lane Primary School

A Day In The Life Of Indiana Jones

One morning Indiana Jones woke up with a girl in bed. He woke her up and both of them went into the girl's bedroom where they found a passageway. It looked like it led to Egypt. They went a long way through the passage and came to a door. They opened the door and it was full of bugs. They went through another door and found a trap. The girl found a doorway and Indiana Jones said, 'Thank you.'
The girl said, 'That's alright.'
They went a very, very long way into the special cave where they found several scary bears. The girl screamed loud and long and the noisy bears ran away.

Five minutes later a small girl appeared from the other side of the cave. She was crying for her mum who had been locked in a dungeon. Indiana and the girl rescued the little girl's mum and made their way back the same way as they'd come. At the end of the passage they stepped back into Indiana Jones' bedroom. He slammed the door and pulled the lever, locking the door forever.

Kayleigh McFarland (9)
Field Lane Primary School

THE VAMPIRE MYSTERY

One day there was a girl walking down an alleyway when a spooky thing happened to her. A man jumped out on her and shouted, 'Boo!' It was very scary at the time and that night, she bravely walked back down the alleyway again. The man was there again and he jumped out and shouted, 'Boo!' This time she was really scared so she ran back home and told her mum and dad.

The next day when the girl was walking to school, she walked straight past the alleyway and glanced, and saw the man. He was definitely the same person. He looked like a vampire. There was a police station over the road so she went to the police and she gave them a description of him. At first they didn't believe her and they went out to see if it was true or not. The man was gone! It was very strange. The policeman and woman didn't believe her, but that night one of the policemen came out and found the man who was stood waiting for the girl near the alleyway. The policeman just glanced at the man.

Later that night the policeman looked at the description that the girl had given him and yes, it was the man that scared the girl. The next day they took the man away and the girl lived happily ever after.

Melissa Jayne Hrab (9)
Field Lane Primary School

A Spooky Story

One dark and spooky night, Robert was playing on his computer. He looked at the back of his game and it said 'Monsters And Mummies Of Mayhem!' He started playing on it when suddenly his computer went multicoloured. He shouted, 'Mum!' but it was too late, he was in the computer. He found himself on the first level. It was silent.

Argh he was surrounded by ninjas and then a sword appeared in his hands so he chopped, chopped and chopped and soon he was at the next level. There was a sound and big sharp buildings appeared. It was Egypt. He got a shotgun. *Bang! Bang! Bang!* When there were mummies, he had to hit them on the head. *Argh!* The sand was blowing in his face. What was happening?

Things were happening so fast and he was going to the next level. It was the city. Zombies started following him, he got an axe. *Chop, chop, chop*. All the zombies were dead. He jumped out of the computer and he never played on it again.

Ben Shryane (9)
Field Lane Primary School

A Day In The Life Of A Polar Bear

In the icy cold Arctic there were two polar bears. One was a king polar bear and the other one was a queen polar bear. They had creamy white fur, big black eyes and a black nose and were both nineteen years old.

One morning the queen told the king to go out and find some food so he did. When he came out of his ice house, he suddenly sank in the snow, it was quite deep but he managed to get out.

Eventually he got to a small breathing hole. He waited and waited so he sat down. A while later he saw something move in the water, he stood up and got ready. Up came a seal and he snatched it.
The seal squeaked, 'If you let me go, I will give you three wishes.'
The polar bear said, 'Really!'
'Really,' said the seal.
So he let him go and ran back to the ice house and a surprise was waiting. The queen had had three cubs and they were the most cutest things.
The queen said, 'Where's the food?'
The king replied that the seal had granted him three wishes so they tried to make a wish, it didn't work. That seal had cheated them.

The polar bears were really angry so they both went with the cubs on their backs to wait for a while. They saw a few seals, one popped up, then another and they caught five and then the one that had cheated them and they lived a very happy life.

Dominic Siekierkowski (10)
Harewood CE Primary School

A Day In The Life Of Mr Bean

Mr Bean awoke, said hello to his teddy and went downstairs. He went down to wash his suit and trousers but when he arrived the washing machine was broken. Mr Bean grabbed his teddy and washing and went to the laundrette. When he arrived, he put his washing into the machine and waited. He murmured to his teddy, 'I wonder what's for tea?' *Bing*, the washing machine had finished, he gathered it up, except a sock at the back of the machine. Mr Bean climbed into the dark, dingy washing machine to grab his sock, while doing this an old wrinkly woman shut the door behind him (it was a accident because she didn't see him).

The machine went into washing mode, it was frantically spinning and foaming up onto the window. It then went into spin mode, whirling round and around. It made Mr Bean feel sick, weary and dizzy. It slowed down to dry and got sweltering hot. (Mr Bean started to roast like a roast chicken. Teddy thought he could have him for tea.)

The wrinkly old woman came back, let Mr Bean out, he rolled out into his washing. At that moment, the sock dropped onto his nose and the old wrinkly woman looked at Mr Bean in a peculiar way. Mr Bean picked up his washing, walked off in the most curvy line, put teddy on the seat and drove off in his lime-green Mini. That night he said to teddy that it had been a horrible, extraordinary day.

Thomas Crocker-Pleasant (11)
Harewood CE Primary School

THE SECRET HOUSE ON THE COAST

A few days ago there was a girl, she was thirteen, her name was Clare. She was not a nice girl at all, but one day . . .

Clare went outside, she could not sleep so she went for some air but the ghosts of the coast came and killed her, or so they thought . . . but she was a ghost. She flashed into the darkness and just then she was outside a house. She walked inside, the door shut quickly and then she saw a Roman. He was young, not a child but an adult.
'Well you are the same as me, you are a ghost and you will get used to it. I am trying to get out of here! Come on we can find our way out of this . . . ' he said.
There was a pause, something was mumbling, it was a huge metal ball. The Roman got Clare by the arm and ran to another room. It was a dormitory.
'All right, is this house booby trapped?' said Clare.
'Yes!' said the Roman and off they went.

The Roman saw some ghosts on the TV in the pink room, it was like a chat show. Clare and the Roman went into another room, it was circular. In there was a group of people.
'Oh no,' said the Roman, it was a death room.
The ceiling was getting lower and lower. Clare tried to run out of the room with the Roman but the door was locked. Clare noticed a trapdoor where the floor was, she went through the door and found that she was home. The Roman was dead as he never got out of the house.

Tesfya Gorebooth (10)
Harewood CE Primary School

THE SCHOOL'S SECRET ROOM

'I must not be rude to teachers . . .' wrote Jane.
'I must not play ball before school', wrote Joe.
The clock ticked on, at last their detention was over. The teacher packed up and said goodbye. The school was deserted, not a thing moved. Jane was scared but Joe was excited.

The school was silent until a knock came clearly from underneath their feet. Jane ran out the big front door, screaming loudly. She was followed closely by Joe. He was not screaming but his face was deadly white.
'What was that?' panted Jane
'I'm not sure!' Joe replied. 'We were on the ground floor and it came from below.'

They very bravely went back inside thinking the same thing *(this place must be haunted).* Joe was new to the school and switched the forbidden switch! The floor rumbled and split, revealing steps. They climbed down and saw a sight to be remembered. Hundreds and hundreds of ghosts, some small, some big, some that looked rich or poor but all the tall ones had smiles on their faces. Once they had got over the shock (both the ghosts and the children), they made friends. It turned out that the ghosts were lonely so they knocked to see if anyone would come. They made friends and every night, even if they didn't have detention, Jane and Joe played with the ghosts. The ghosts may still live there but I do not know.

Lorna Hulse (11)
Harewood CE Primary School

A DAY IN THE LIFE OF FRANKIE DETTORI

Frankie Dettori awoke in the morning to get ready for his seven races at Royal Ascot. When he arrived in his helicopter, he asked Sheikh Mohammed how to ride his horse and then went off to meet his horses' owners and trainers. He then went and got changed for the first race and practised on the mechanical horse.

Later on Frankie was ready for his first race on Wall Street. After winning his first race of the day it led him to get the magnificent seven. He managed to make everyone happy, cheering him on, even the other jockeys were congratulating him even though he had just beaten them all.

The horses that he won with were called: Wall Street (Cumberland Lodge Stakes), Diffident (Diadem Stakes), Decorated Hero (Tote Festival Handicap), Mark Of Esteem (QE2 Stakes), Fatefully (Rosemary Rated Stakes), Lochangel (Blue Seal Conditions Stakes) and Fujiyama Crest (Gordon Carter Handicap).

Later, after he'd been congratulated by everyone and said goodbye, he got all his gear and set off in his helicopter back home. When he got there, he had a sandwich and watched every single victory on video to see how much he had won by and to make sure he had not dreamt his day of wins. When he had had a little rest, he started putting all seven cups away.

Imran Ali (10)
Harewood CE Primary School

HOUSE NUMBER 13

Inside the scary, spooky, smelly house something stirred. Among the dust so thickly layered, there was a misty floating thing. Whatever could it be? It was pure white and had no smell. The thing rose and with it, from the most peculiar spaces (including the toilet) thousands and thousands of the same white floating things rose as well. Meanwhile Ben and Frank were doing some research on that particular house that was supposedly haunted (Number 13).

They found out that on Friday the 13th of June, 2003, an old lady had sold her house and no one had moved in.

Ben was a well-built person who worn jeans and a hooded jumper. Frank was just about the same because they were twins, they enjoyed playing football and were usually found playing football on the large wall outside the spooky house as they called it. But one day the ball was given an almighty kick by Ben and flew straight into the spooky house.

They entered the house and headed straight into an open window where they found a ball, they picked it up and it exploded! It was a water bomb, they found a stick and poked all the balls which they found. Half an hour later, they found their ball and ran out quickly.

Now after that experience, they were not willing to go back in and do it again, they had their ball and that was all they cared about. Nothing was stirring, or was it? Only time will tell.

Richard Moore (11)
Harewood CE Primary School

A Day In The Life Of My Mum

It's early in the morning and my mum is going to have a typical day. Waking up, practically asleep while brushing her teeth. Going downstairs, having her normal tea and cereal, spilling nearly all of it on the kitchen table, having to make another cup.

Then she has to drop us kids off at school (after finally getting us out of the house). She has to make yet another journey to work (yawn). My mum parks her car near a college. I mean who would want to go there?

My mum works for Leeds City Council, Customer Services, you know people with problems. She's stressed by the fourth customer. The waiting line, oww, you have to wait up to an hour. My mum says, 'You still have to serve them in a nice friendly manner,' (yeah, yeah).

When work is over she comes and picks us up from school which is twenty minutes and then fifteen minutes to get back home, (blah, blah, blah).

My mum has the big list of: washing up, cleaning, hovering, making dinner, cleaning up again. When it finally comes to an end (as she says) she just needs to make a quick cup of tea, then relax and watch a movie with my dad, (you don't want to know about his day). I don't see what work she has to do?

Sanjeet Choda (11)
Harewood CE Primary School

A Day In The Life Of Lenny Henry

A day in the life of Lenny Henry is exciting, because he's funny. When Lenny wakes up, he does all the usual things like: breakfast, brush teeth, get dressed. When he finishes, he goes downstairs and reads the paper.

When he's about to leave, he hears, 'Bye Lenny,' shouts Dawn. When he tries to open the door, he can't because it's locked and he can't find the keys. He knows he has to be quick because he has to practise for Comic Relief, because he's the main person. He's running all over the place just to find those keys. He stops for a second to think where he put them. *Where did I leave them last night?* Ten minutes later he finds them behind the telephone.

Once he gets in the car, he has to speed like mad to get to the show. He's speeding down the roads, people think he's a maniac. When he is very nearly there, he hits a hen on the side of the road. After that, he says, 'I wonder what we're having for tea?'

When he gets there, the producer says, 'You're late.'
Lenny replies, 'I stopped to help an animal on the road.'

When he gets home, he eats chicken tikka for tea, then he watches some TV and after, he goes upstairs to read his book. It was the best day ever. (I hope I don't become famous.)

James Hartley (11)
Harewood CE Primary School

THE 15TH CENTURY MANSION GHOST

Creak! Slowly somewhere a door was being opened. Kelly woke up suddenly. She wondered what that noise was and where it was from. She thought it could have been from the 15th century mansion down the street she lives on. *If in the morning I wake up early, I'll wake up Joe. We can go and explore the mansion,* Kelly wondered.

Time passed and morning came. Kelly woke to find her mum, dad and her brother Joe were already awake. Kelly was always the first one up. She got changed, brushed her teeth and ran as fast as she could downstairs. She looked out of a window to see if there was anyone near the mansion. She slowly walked into the kitchen like nothing had happened, and poured her cereal.
'All right, Kelly love?' asked Mum. 'It looked as though you were in a rush for something and it isn't there.'
'No, I'm fine,' Kelly answered.

At about 7 o'clock, Kelly and Joe went to explore the mansion and when they opened the door, it was smelly and it looked really ancient. *Bang!* 'What was that?' Kelly muttered in shock.
'Probably just . . . a ghost!' Joe screamed.
Kelly looked behind herself and she saw a ghost. Kelly saw a very old ghost washer she had seen in a book. She told Joe, and they sucked up the ghost and nailed a plank of wood on the lid.

Kelly and Joe ran home and told Mum, but she didn't believe them, so they kept it a secret until it was absolutely necessary to tell someone. They wondered if the ghost could escape?

Manpreet Ryatt (10)
Harewood CE Primary School

THE ELECTRIC FIRE

It was a warm day and I was just coming home from school, when my friend ran up to me and said, 'Would you like to go to the park?'
'Yes,' I said.
'Let's go then.'

When we got there it was three o'clock in the afternoon and my friend Olivia had a metal belt on. First we went on the merry-go-round, then we went on the seesaw. I thought I was going to fall off! Last of all, we went on the slide. I went on first, it was great fun and very fast. Then Olivia went on the slide.

The slide had an electric circuit running through it, but the circuit was not complete, however Olivia was wearing a metal belt. Olivia got onto the slide and slid down. Suddenly, the circuit became complete and Olivia got an electric shock, but also, the wires got hot and a fire started at the bottom of the slide. The bright red flames engulfed Olivia until they grew so fierce that Olivia could not see through them.

The flames grew thicker and thicker, smoke was rising into the sky. Olivia was spluttering, but then I realised what to do. I knew I could not use water to extinguish the fire because it was an electric fire. So I took off my jumper and hit the fire with it. The fire went out slowly and Olivia was rescued.

As we drove safely away in the ambulance that I had called, I saw a flickering flame . . .

Uzair Khan (8)
Harewood CE Primary School

A GAS FIRE

I was driving in the new jeep with my mum, quite slowly so that the car didn't run out of petrol. We had to make it to the petrol station behind the old pub. After about five minutes we got there. My mum gave me some money to go and buy sweets with, but I waited until she came with me. I watched her take the nozzle out of the tank and just at that very moment, I saw someone pull into the petrol station (in a Porsche Boxter) my mum stopped. She saw a man's head through his car window.

The man got out of his Porsche and then walked by. When he came back, he accidentally spilt petrol and it was heading in my mum's direction, and if matters couldn't get any worse, he was lighting a match at the same time for his cigarette and a big ball of fire shot towards my mum. It sent my mum flying backwards. My mum was just lying on the concrete floor. She was surrounded by fire! What was I going to do about it?

I went up to my mum (as close as I could, of course, because she was surrounded by fire.) I checked whether she was breathing. She was breathing (her stomach went up like a hill and down like a cake that's gone wrong.) The man in the Porsche left after he'd seen what had happened, I think he'd burnt his hand or something. I went back up to my mum, I stood and shouted her name . . . there was no response. I got out my mobile, but I realised that I had no credit on my phone. At that moment, I could have cried . . . I thought that emergency calls were free! So I called the police. I told them where I was and who I was with.

After about ten to fifteen minutes, the police came with an ambulance and they got my mum out of the fire. They said she would be OK. They gave me a lift to my dad's house and they kept my mum in hospital. She came back about three days later, completely recovered!

Olivia Feldman (9)
Harewood CE Primary School

FIRE IN THE FLAT

I was walking down the street to see my big brother Max. When I got to the flat, I knocked. There was no answer. I knocked again, still no answer. I found the door was unlocked, so I went in. Suddenly, flames were all around me. I ran and ran until I was out of the flat. I looked around, I saw a phone box and I rang the fire brigade.

Ten minutes later, the fire brigade arrived and so did an ambulance. The fire brigade were having problems putting the fire out, but just then, it started to rain, thunder and lightning. *Boom! Crash! Boom! Crash!* The fire people were very glad that it had started to rain, because it would help to put the fire out. The advisors said that petrol was poured through the letterbox and milk bottles had been thrown through the window. I was horrified at the sound of that.

The fire seemed to be dying down. In about ten minutes, some fire people went in and came out with Max. The doctor said he'd be fine.

Jordan Appleson (8)
Harewood CE Primary School

OVEN'S ALERT

It was a Tuesday, a warm summer's day. Me and Tania were walking to my car because Tania was coming to my house. We were quite thirsty, so we went into the Harewood Arms for a drink of water each. As we sat down, I noticed smoke coming from underneath the door. We decided to go and investigate.

When we opened the door, we had to step to the side because there was a sudden rush of chefs with red faces. One of the ovens was on fire. We went in, carefully, but Tania slipped. The bump made some of the fire fall onto the floor and form a fire hoop around her.

I ran to find a phone, but the smoke was too thick and I was so worried about Tania. I went back to see how Tania was. She wasn't breathing! I started sweating like I was running a 500-mile marathon. I was getting very scared and very worried.

It was getting very dramatic. I heard the door open. I turned around and looked aimlessly. It was Mum! I showed her to Tania. She called 999 on her mobile phone for a fire engine and an ambulance. At five o'clock,
when the emergency services had gone and Tania was OK, I drove Tania home, because she was still slightly ill.

Two weeks later she was fully recovered.

Sophie White (8)
Harewood CE Primary School

THE CURSE

The Scene

It was Friday the thirteenth of June, 2003 at four-thirty, when two boys called Jack and Oliver decided to explore the forest in Oak Town. The forest had lots of gigantic trees with big walls around it.

The Fire

When Jack and Oliver got near the end of the forest, Jack ran on and he dropped his lantern by accident and it smashed into little tiny pieces. The flame from the candle started a fire and then one of the trees near them fell down in the fire and it created a big wall of flame.

Putting Out The Fire

Oliver called for the fire brigade on his mobile phone, but there was no signal. So he found an old bucket and went to a nearby lake and kept throwing water on the fire, and then finally it went weak and small and Jack jumped over it.

The Curse

When they were running back home to tell what had happened, an old wrinkly man said, 'You know that forest that you have just come out of? That forest is close by evil demons.' Then he turned into a demon.

Then they called the police and sent him back through the door of Hell and they never went back to the forest again.

Jamie Newall (9)
Harewood CE Primary School

THE MOVING STATUE

'Let's check that statue out,' said
Sophie. Sophie and me walked over to the statue.
'Hello,' said the statue, 'can you get me some oil to oil me with?'
'Go and get the oil can, Soph,' I shouted. 'You're a Viking, but aren't you old?'
'A witch in my time put a spell on me so I was frozen for 500 years,' said the Viking statue.
'Come home with me and we'll clean you up,' I said.
Suddenly, Sophie appeared, panting.
'Thanks for the oil, girls, but we'd better go before someone sees me,' said the Viking . . .

By the time we got home it was lunchtime.
'Stay in the art studio and we'll bring you some lunch,' Sophie said.
'Mmm, lunch,' said the Viking hungrily.
'Let's get you dressed and take you back to the park,' Sophie whispered.
'Someone's coming, hide,' I whispered softly.
'I know, let's go through the door to the hallway,' Sophie said.
We climbed up the stairs to the bathroom.
'First, we have to get rid of your beard,' said Sophie.
Zzzzzzzzzzzz
'Perfect,' I said, 'now let's dress you in Dad's old clothes.'
'Brilliant,' Sophie said gladly. 'Let's go.'

When we arrived at the park it was dark.
'We'll miss you,' said Sophie.
'Bye,' we both said, as he climbed onto the pedestal.
'I've had a weird day,' Sophie said.
'Me too,' I said.

Polly-Anna Bury (8)
Harewood CE Primary School

THE MOVING STATUE

When the statue started moving it scared Elliot. Elliot asked him what his name was.
He replied, 'Fred.'
He asked Elliot what his name was.
I said, 'Elliot.'
'Do you have a family?' asked Fred.
'Yes,' said Elliot, 'they are over there. Have you got a family?'
'No.'
'Shall I go and tell my family about you?'
'No,' replied Fred.
'Well what do you want to do?'
'Go and play on the swings,' said Fred.
So they both went to play on the swings.

As soon as they got to the swings Elliot's mother called him. 'Lunchtime,' she said. So Elliot went for his lunch . . .

When he had finished, he found that the statue had gone. So he called to Fred, 'Where are you?'
'I am in the bushes,' Fred said.
'Which bushes?'
'The far ones.'

Elliot went to the far bushes and looked. At last he found him and said, 'I am going now so you had better get back on your pedestal.'
'Bye Elliot, see you soon!'

Elliot Williams (7)
Harewood CE Primary School

A FIRE

It was two o'clock in the afternoon, it was very hot. I went to Wetherby River with my best friend Georgia, we have known each other since we were born.

We were walking along the river, we heard a big bang, we were thinking, *what is happening?* We ran back to the river, two cars had crashed.

I ran to the two cars, the people in the cars were knocked out. I was shouting, 'Are you OK?' I did not hear a thing. The time was five o'clock, smoke was just rising up and up. The colour of the smoke was grey.

We ran for help, we ran into the pub.
I said, 'Please come and help me because there's a crash.'
The man said, 'Yes I will.'
In the end we got the people to the hospital. When I got home my mum was worrying about us. I told her and she was OK about what had happened. I went to the hospital to see the people from the car crash. They thanked me for saving their lives.

When I got home they had sent me flowers. On the card it said 'Thank you for saving our lives, we are best friends'. We now see each other every week at the river at two o'clock every Saturday afternoon until five o'clock and we have fish and chips.

Jessica Walker (8)
Harewood CE Primary School

A Match Fire

I was entering the park with my friend Andrew when we saw Mark on his skateboard.
'Hello loser,' said Mark menacingly. 'Playing with your sissy little friend?'
'Oh shut up!' I said.
Then Andrew and I made a run for the football pitch where two men were playing football.
'Phew, that was close, I thought he was going to beat us up,' said Andrew. 'I'm just going to the toilet,' said Andrew.
'Okay,' I replied.

Andrew walked into the toilets where he saw a tramp dropping a match. Then the tramp walked out smoking a cigarette. Then immediately a fire started!
'Help!' I heard someone shout. At once I raced to the toilets.
'Andrew!' I yelled. Then Mark burst in.
'What have you done now sore loser?' asked Mark.
'Oh never mind that now, but please go and call for an ambulance and the fire brigade.'

It was a few minutes until the ambulance and a fire engine arrived. I told them everything they needed to know. They put out the blazing fire and took Andrew to hospital.

Within a few weeks Andrew came out of hospital with a bandage on his arm where he had burnt himself. On the second day back at school Mark apologised to me for shouting at me in the park, so from that day on me and Mark were best friends.

Hasan Malik (9)
Harewood CE Primary School

The Terrible Accident

One day me and my mum were walking in the woods to the swimming pool at Oasis. We were very happy because we were on holiday together. There were lots of red squirrels going up and down the trees. It was a hot day so we had an ice cream to keep us cool.

'Let's climb up that huge tall tree,' I said to my mum.

We climbed up the huge tall tree, we climbed and climbed, then suddenly my mum fell off the tree. I felt very scared. I didn't know what to do so I climbed back down the tree because I needed to get help.

Then suddenly the torch fell out of my mum's handbag and started a fire. There must have been an electrical fault with it.

I rushed to the swimming pool and got some buckets and filled the buckets with water and rushed back to the fire and put it out. Then I dialled 999 on my mobile phone for an ambulance to pick us up. The paramedics said she had broken her funny bone in her arm, but she would be okay.

Six weeks later when my mum's arm was better we went back to Oasis and enjoyed playing on the flume in the swimming pool!

Simon Moore (8)
Harewood CE Primary School

THE BAD BURN

On the fabulous summer's day I was on my way to the skateboard park with one of my best friends, Katie. It was eleven thirty in the morning. We both sprinted excitedly to the park.

Katie jumped on her skateboard, she whizzed up and down the half-pipe twice. She then did a kick-flip onto the grinding pole, sparks crackled off the board and set fire to a large pile of wood. Katie suddenly lost her balance and fell into the fire. I sat there scared out of my wits.

Trembling I ran, I seized her left leg and I dragged her out of the fire. I saw a huge burn on her right leg. I tried to call 999 from my mobile phone but there was no signal. I didn't know what to do.

After ten to fifteen minutes a policeman walked past. I ran as fast as I could, my heart beating with joy. When I got to the short, smart policeman I stopped.
'Please . . . can . . . you . . . help . . . me? My friend has fallen off her skateboard and has landed in a fire,' I said breathlessly.

I ran back to where Katie was and she showed him her burnt leg. The policeman ordered an ambulance to take us to Harrogate hospital. When we got to the hospital our mums were there, Katie had been taken to a room, so my mum asked me what happened. I explained. She was pleased that nothing more serious had happened.

Leah Feldman (9)
Harewood CE Primary School

A FIRE

One super day, me and Callum went to Harewood House for a bank holiday treat. We got a delicious ice cream each topped with two flakes. Suddenly the van tipped up and some petrol came out. A boy made a spark by scraping his chain on his trousers against the ground and the spark went on the petrol and made a three-foot wide fire.

We sprinted as fast as we could. Suddenly Callum tripped up over a stone and the fire went on him. I carried on. Then I found a house so I knocked on the door. Someone familiar came out. 'Elliot,' I shouted, 'come with me.'

We both ran to Callum and helped him up.
'Oh no, Elliot's gone,' I said. I went back and took him to Callum. I got my mobile phone out and rang the ambulance to come.

One hour later the ambulance came and I helped them put Elliot and Callum on stretchers. They were very heavy. When we had put them on we went to the hospital. Our mums picked us up there. Luckily they were not too hurt.

Michael Gregson (8)
Harewood CE Primary School

TO THE BITTER END

The clash of Elven steel against Orc scimitar, the wail and moaning of the dead. The skies crashed, the heavens opened, death soared about like a vulture to its carcass. Shrieks came from the foul, evil Orcs as an Elven hero leapt into the ranks, swaying his sword to and fro like a pendulum, but his match then came.

An Orc warlord charged forward, this one bore crude armour and an expression like death. It stared at the glittering elf for a seemingly endless time, its bloodshot eyes transfixed on the elf hero. It then gave a banshee wail and threw itself in. The first blow hit the elf's shoulder, a vein was cut and a river of blood came out. The elf made a hard stroke, laying sparks into the air, but the second one hit the Orc's face and a blood and slime-covered eye tumbled to the ground. The Orc screamed and fell to the floor, quivering. Then it suddenly leapt up, stuck a knife in the elf's chest and hit him. The elf stumbled about, dazed and wounded. The Orc lunged forward but two Elven arrows halted his advance. The dazed elf recovered and attacked, but suddenly stopped, he looked at his gut, a huge Orc scimitar was sticking through it, its cruel blade piercing the heart. The elf lurched back and died. The Orc cackled in blood-red sky, the battlefield choked with lifeless bodies. Who cared about his dead Orcs anyway? It was dinnertime.

Soon after, the field was silent; the only sound was the carrion crows and the scavenging wolves, feasting to their heart's content. This was the horror of war, the death of heroes, the massacre of thousands and the fear of what was next to come . . .

William Lord (11)
Leeds Grammar School

HEAVEN FOR HELL

James Stevenson didn't see or feel the van that hit him. One minute he was running over Oxford Street with a stack of CDs in his hand and the clang of the alarm bell in his ears and the next, nothing.

That was the trouble with shoplifting of course, once you were caught you had to go for it, and you couldn't stop for such niceties as looking left or right. James had gone for it and he had not made it!

'Blimey this isn't happening,' he croaked, unless this was a hallucination he wasn't in London. The only difference was there were no shops only clouds and a big golden gate. There was a long queue stretching as far as he could see. People were waiting as if they expected it to happen.
Then this voice yelled, 'I want to see James Stevenson right now.'
James ran as fast as he could and got there a minute later, there was a man, a man who wouldn't have looked out of place at the North Pole. He was wearing a long robe. James then realised he had been killed.

'James,' the man said, 'how old are you?'
'Fifteen,' James replied.
'Why weren't you at school?'
'It was a training day.'
'Right in you go.'

James obediently entered and found he was wearing a robe. 'I want to go to Hell!' James complained, looked up and saw something unusual on the man's head.
The Devil turned around grinning, 'Did you think you went to Heaven in the first place?'

Robert Hooley (11)
Leeds Grammar School

THE RUN FROM THE HOUSE

Earlier, I was playing tennis with my dad when my mobile went off. I had received a text message. It said, 'U will die 2night'.
I showed it to my dad who was as amazed as me. I could now wait forever until tonight.
'Help, help me Dad,' I pleaded.

The rest of the day passed without anything else strange happening, and we knew we had to get out of the house. It sounded though they had broken the conservatory so we had to get to the front door another way round.

On the way there my dad picked up the cricket bat. Luckily there was only one enemy, who my dad hit over the head with the bat. I picked up the crowbar he was carrying just in case we came across someone else. Then we saw something we did not want to see. Outside, running towards the conservatory were two men with machine guns. Both were firing at the already-wrecked conservatory. Then I realised they weren't firing at the conservatory but at me. The only thing we could do was run out and get onto the main road.

When we got there we rang the police. They went to the house and sorted it all out. When we got home everything was smashed. I dashed to my room to check that the laptop hadn't been found, and ran straight in to hear three bullets fired . . .

Sam Grant (11)
Leeds Grammar School

GHOST CREEK

It was September 1st, 1997. My friends Sam, Jonathan and James and I had just moved into a large, scary-looking mansion near this river creek. We were college students and this was our apartment. We thought it was a good house in the catalogue but we should have looked first in 'Britain's Most Haunted Houses.'

Anyway, it was the first night it started to get to me. I was asleep in my new room when a noise in the hall woke me up. A sudden chill crept up my spine as I got out of bed and peered round the door. A white glowing shape of a man was staggering into Sam's dormitory. I was scared, but I had to do something. I ran into his room to find the worst shock of my life. I screamed and shouted bringing Jonathan and James running, making them paralysed with shock. There, pinned on the wall by a spear was Sam. Next to him, written in his own blood were the words, *'Leave now, you are next!'* I tried to call the police but the phone wires were cut and my mobile was dead. We stayed together that night, too scared to get any sleep.

The next morning we ate breakfast out at a restaurant. We sat around the table and thought up ways to get rid of the ghost but they were all crazy. Then it hit me. If the ghost walked but didn't float, we could drown him in the creek! That night we put my plan into action. We left James sitting by the creek as bait. Sure enough he came, limping along. He looked like a zombie from the Tudor times, with tights, long hair and a beard. When he was closest to the river we sprang out from the rock and shouted at him. With surprise he toppled and splash-less fell into the murky depths of the river. We all cheered but James started to scream. A large, warty hand had grabbed his leg and pulled him into the river and he drowned.

We had a police investigation but they could only offer a funeral service. I am telling this six years later to warn you. Stay away from Ghost Creek. Spirits live and they are after you!

Matthew McGoldrick (11)
Leeds Grammar School

A Day In Baghdad

8.30am Tuesday 11th February, 2003

We are in our attacking position ready for the general to give us the nod and blow Saddam Hussein into oblivion!

9am

We have started to proceed towards the Baghdad gates where the first line of Iraqi troops wait for us.

10am

The sound of guns is ringing in my head and the bellows of the troops falling to the ground in grief. We are slowly ploughing through the Iraqi resistance.

10.02am

I have just lost the best friend of my life and those Iraqis are going to pay for it.

11am

We have received back-up from the 21st Infantry Division. The first line is now on the floor, giving us a gateway through to the city centre.

11.30am

Thousands of Iraqi troops have formed up in front of us blocking our path. Our only choice is to hit them with all we have got.

3pm

There is blood flying everywhere and we are being slaughtered by Iraqis. This is much harder than I expected.

4.30pm

We started off with about 2,000 troops, we have now been whittled down to 600. We have no choice but to start retreating.

5pm

All that has happened is that 50 more English soldiers have been murdered and the surviving troops have gone back 150m. We are really trying to get back but there is no clear cut ways through without being shot.

6pm

The sirens are now wailing, bombs drop from the air and . . .

Dominic Wrench (11)
Leeds Grammar School

BENEATH THE SURFACE

Deep, deep down on the bed of the lake not a thing moves. It is as silent as the grave. It is so cold it makes your bones ache. The darkness is as black as ink. In the silky layer of mud something metal, rusty and twisted stuck up through the silt and seaweed. A handlebar of a tricycle was half buried in the thick, slimy ooze. Look closer and gripping tightly to the handlebar, five little bones of a child's hand.

Let me take you back to a warm summer's day in 1917, during the Great War. There was a blazing sun in the sky and the buzz of bees mumbling around the roses filled the air. Henry's mother decided that it was far too nice to stay indoors doing homework, so she packed up a picnic of Marmite sandwiches, Henry's favourite chocolate biscuits and some Ribena. She said that they would go to Roundhay Park. They could play on the swings and feed the ducks on the lake. Just as they were ready to go Henry asked if he could bring his tricycle. She said that he could as long as he did not ride too far ahead.

On their way she stopped at the newsagents to buy a newspaper. She put it in her basket and they walked on. When they reached the park they found the big tree where they always had their picnics. His mother sat down and Henry rode off towards the swings on his tricycle. She pulled out her newspaper and started to read all the news about the war. On the front page there was a picture of a soldier and underneath it said, 'Hero killed in action'. Henry's mother stared at it for a couple of minutes and then let out a huge scream! She jumped up knocking over the picnic basket and forgetting all about Henry, his mother ran out of the park with tears streaming down her face.

Soon Henry got bored of the swings so he rode back up to the big tree to find his mother, but she was not there. He turned around and then he saw a man in a khaki uniform waving to him. 'Daddy,' he shouted. Henry started pedalling frantically down the slipway towards the man.

He was reaching quite high speeds now and he tried to brake by putting his feet out, but it did not work. Just as he reached the bottom of the slipway the man disappeared into thin air.

The cold, black waters of the lake closed over Henry's head as he sank into its murky, black depths.

Jonathan Letts (11)
Leeds Grammar School

MI6 ATTACK!

It was 2000CE on the eleventh month, the sixth day at 1400 hours. Agent R Morgan - or Cheetah, to use his code name - had reported to his boss and was discussing the matter of nuclear waste.

'You see Cheetah,' it was the MI6 boss speaking, 'we fear that nuclear waste is being stored and processed into a bomb.'
'I'll find it then,' replied Cheetah, 'and take care of those terrorists while I'm at it.'
'Yes, well . . .' it was a worker at MI6 speaking, ' . . . it seems . . . well, they've found us!'
Boom! The door was blown open. Cheetah called his assistant Wolf and they picked up their handguns and ran to the balcony above the entrance hall, but when the terrorists shot back with rifles, Cheetah and Wolf retreated to a corridor. Cheetah and Wolf equipped their gadgets and continued to fight.

'*Go!*' shouted Cheetah and they ran past a group of five enemies leaving behind a bomb disguised as a cigarette. Just then they were surrounded.
'Vop vor veapons,' a terrorist with a twisted face said.
'Think we can take 'em?' whispered Wolf to Cheetah.
'"Course,' replied Cheetah before throwing a smoke bomb and attacking Wolf. Cheetah and Wolf shot the terrorists as they gasped for air until their ammo ran out, kicked them until their legs got tired, punched until their arms got tired, headbutted until their heads became sore and bit necks until the smoke had cleared and the last terrorist was down.

'Threat eliminated,' said the computer.

Robert Morgan (11)
Leeds Grammar School

HOOKED UP?

I decided to go fishing one day and I caught five fish and I had them for tea.

When I got up the next Monday morning I read in the newspapers about the 'Hooker', a man who was murdering people. So I read the article and a man had been hooked up through the throat, hanging from the main entrance to his flats. I threw away the paper and tried to not look sick.

The papers kept on finding people hanging somewhere by a hook piercing their body parts in a painful, bloody death like a war. Everyone was worried so we all went to the town hall to discuss the matter and the judge had picked someone at random and accused them and gave them the death penalty because the judge was going mad. Then he picked someone next to me and gave him the death penalty.

When we went to court the next morning the judge was hanging from his eye sockets, bleeding. The police decided that they would check every house for hooks and other items.

Then the next morning all the police squads were in a group tied together with all of them having a hook down their throats, impaling their flesh like the spikes of a 400-pound syringe.

After all the people in the town had died tragic deaths, except the babies who had been left to rot and die like opened-up apples, I moved on to the next town to murder them.

Richard Limb (11)
Leeds Grammar School

TITANIC

Hello, my name is Ronald Juniper and this is my account of the sea disaster I experienced.

It all started when I was in the bar. I was chatting to my wife and my daughter, Alexandra, who was about 17. We were talking about how safe this ship was, but we were wrong.

My wife Charlotte went back to the cabin to get her coat when she noticed her bed had moved about a metre and was nearly touching the back of the cabin. This was very odd. Then my wife fell over because the floor was going upwards.

When she came back she told me what had happened. Suddenly a little boy of about 5 shouted, 'The boat is sinking.' No one believed him. Then everybody laughed.
Then the officer on board came in and shouted, 'It's true, we are going to die!'

I panicked, my wife and my daughter got in a boat and disappeared into the horizon. I thought I would never see them again. This was the lucky part. I actually got into a lifeboat and before I knew it I was off as quick as David Beckham running up and down a football pitch.

The sight was dreadful. I saw that the ship had gone down into the dark ocean. My heart sank in desperation for the poor people left on the ship. I had to row for hours. I remembered that the gentleman sitting beside me kept throwing up over the side of the boat.

Suddenly I heard a massive cheer. I looked behind me and saw a big boat. One man on my boat shouted, 'The ship has come to rescue us.' I felt relieved.

Marco Sarussi (11)
Leeds Grammar School

THE WAR AGAINST BRITAIN, A GERMAN POINT OF VIEW

'Quick, get out the tanks,' said General Rommel. 'Ve are at var.'

Panic surged in my head. My name is Hans Hommerstadt, a new member of the 8th Panzer Division. This was Hitler's plan: divide the army and attack the British in groups of about 50 and in particular Vinston Churchill, if possible.

'Come on, get a move on Hans.'
'Going as quick as I can,' I replied to whoever had called me. 'Her engine is too cold, she needs to get varmed up.'

Finally, the engine reached a suitable temperature and my crew and I climbed in the tank and set off to fight the British. No one knew how big the British army was, or even if this was the army and not just a division, like us.

Suddenly, British tanks came roaring over the hill like liquid in a saucepan that had been on the heat too long. They had about 150 tanks whereas we had 95.
Then Rommel's voice came on the radio. 'All crews, I vant you to fire two bullets at the British, on my vistle, *now!*'

It worked. About 50 of their tanks exploded and after that, war had broken out. Everybody was firing shells, machine guns, flame-throwers and whatever they could to force the enemy to retreat. There were two hours of non-stop battle where nearly everyone got hit by something or other.

Eventually though we came through, we forced the British to retreat and the whole army celebrated! It was one of the best parties I've ever had. The whole army stayed up late into the night and drank and laughed and talked as much as they could. It was the best feeling in the world!

Michael Ballmann (11)
Leeds Grammar School

THE HOUSEKEEPER

Down near Coventry lived a rich family called the McGraths. They lived in a big, scary manor.

One day in spring in 1757, Alice McGrath (the mother) was mourning in her bedroom after the recent death of her husband, Edmund. When she came back downstairs she noticed that outside the housekeeper was hanging the washing out, but the only key for the door was in Alice's pocket and the windows didn't open. After that, Alice kept a sharp, cutting eye on the housekeeper's every move, but the housekeeper, who I will now refer to as Miss Spiker, noticed this and realised that people cannot watch you with their eyes shut, if that person is asleep or they are not there to watch you.

On the first Sunday before Easter, Alice went to church without the children so Miss Spiker took this as an advantage. She was out picking apples and planned to put Alice under a lot of pressure and make her very unhappy. She would tie a rope onto the apple tree and put a loop in it and place a stool directly underneath it. Have you guessed? She was going to hang Tom, Alice's youngest son, though he would do most of the work himself.

Tom stood on the stool to get a nice juicy apple, but he couldn't quite reach. So, to get further forward Tom put his head in the loop then, with the mind of Satan, Miss Spiker kicked the stool away.

Miss Spiker had vanished off the face of the Earth and all of this happening at once was too much. Alice couldn't cope, so she took a knife to her throat and felt the cold steel touching her fresh, red blood.

Alistair Finerty (11)
Leeds Grammar School

MY WORST DAY OUT

We set off for Gatwick at the start of our holiday to Spain and we were very excited. My sister who is seven was annoying me and started biting me.
My dad told us off and said, 'Stop acting like babies.' My dad was not in a good mood and started to lose control of the car. My mum told my dad to concentrate.

My sister started biting me and in one moment my dad turned round. He lost control of the car and hit a wall.
I shouted, 'Noooooooo!'

Swiftly my parents were rushed to hospital. They were treated immediately. After an hour the doctor pulled me aside into the relatives room.
The first thing I said was, 'Are they alright?'
The doctor said, 'I am sorry, neither of them made it.'
Tears started to drip down my eyes. I was shivering and distraught.

After what I thought was going to be a good few days, it turned out to be a disaster. After a week living with my gran, two people adopted me and took me off to Ethiopia. I did not want to leave. It would be tough in Ethiopia. I had to scavenge for food and drink and worst of all, I did not like the people looking after me.

Day in, day out, I was crying saying, 'I want my parents back; I just want my parents back.' I knew they would not come back, I just needed to get on with my life in Africa, which turned out to be a very dreadful one.

I caught a very bad disease called AIDS and was told I was only going to live for a further two years then join my parents in Heaven.

Edward Dean (11)
Leeds Grammar School

THE WAR GAME

Thud! I heard as a gun dropped from a newly killed man. The war had been going on for two months. We started with 50,000 men, now we have only 700 left. We are outnumbered by hundreds, but we will fight to the death if need be.

I was out of ammo for my P2K so I switched to my AK47. Luckily there was an explosive tanker behind so I aimed carefully then shot without hesitation.
'Nice shot soldier,' my sergeant said to me.
'Thanks Sarge,' I replied.
Just then a German soldier killed my sergeant.
'I'm English and I'm proud of it,' I angrily replied.

Suddenly he blew up my transport.
Then I angrily said, 'OK, now it's personal.' So I got my CH6 rocket launcher and blew his head clear off his shoulders.

Our troop moved into the centre to try and invade their base. Suddenly another troop of Germans surrounded us. We were unable to shoot anywhere where there would not be return fire.

'I've got an idea,' I said. I used my phone to call for air transport straight away. When it came I was the last one to climb aboard. I pulled the top off a grenade and dropped it right where we were standing. *Boom!* As the grenade went off.

The skies looked clear until a German bomber entered the scene. We shot at it like crazy until it was out of the air. Then we reached the base, pushed past the guards and destroyed the base. Then the guns fell silent and peace was restored.

Alex Walden (11)
Leeds Grammar School

FOOTBALL FEVER

One hot, sunny day John and Peter were playing football. They heard growling noises and tiptoed across to the trees near their play den. As they walked into the clearing they heard a roaring of thunder and flashes of dazzling light.

When they opened their eyes, they found themselves in a jungle. Whilst walking they could hear sounds like animals that live in the jungle that began to get louder and louder, until a cloud of smoke and then, silence.

When the smoke had cleared all the animals had gathered around them. A group of monkeys stood next to them. Suddenly some of the monkeys grabbed hold of them and pulled them in a westerly direction. When they came to a standstill, a man appeared, well it looked like a man. Nondescript face, short body, around 3ft long arms, but normal feet. We all stood there and gazed at the stranger.

After a few minutes he began to speak. 'My friends, get me the treasure and I will grant you both three wishes.' They were both so scared they didn't know what else to do, but agree to carry out the instructions.

As they approached the river they could see a bridge and carefully crossed it. The treasure appeared just inside a cavern. John picked up the treasure, raced back over the bridge, turned to look at Peter to express his joy at retrieving the treasure, all he could see was an empty bridge.

Gemma Boyle (10)
St Nicholas RC Primary School, Leeds

THE SUPERHEROES

For Michael and his twin sister Claire, life was boring. For a start their hair was dull-brown and their eyes were no better. Michael was short, fat and always chewed ferociously on his fingernails. Claire was tall, thin and wouldn't even think of chewing on hers. They got picked on at school, not only for those reasons, but that they were rich and had bodyguards trudging around after them.

Their parents were famous actors and every night they disappeared with their big sister Robin, they would come back at dawn. Then in the papers Cat-Man, Cat-Woman and The Raging Robin had arrested some villains like Lady Viper and Sergeant Superglue.

It now was midnight and the twins were telling ghost stories from a very scary book, with an expensive Burberry blanket, but they weren't telling ghost stories, they were plotting.

In their house there were three floors, two of them the twins knew, but they were restricted from the third. They knew that the moonlight rendezvous would go on for at least another two hours, so they tiptoed cautiously into the hall and climbed the winding staircase up to the forbidden third floor. What they say had them bewildered. Suits for the greatest superheroes that they knew! Cat-Man, Cat-Woman and The Raging Robin were there. Someone stepped up behind them, it was Dad. He said in his deep, booming, giant-like voice, 'It's time for you to start training!'

Joseph Geddes (10)
St Nicholas RC Primary School, Leeds

MOVING HOUSE

It was a dull, rainy Monday morning as I walked to the car. Me and my mum had to move into a new house around the corner. When we arrived at the house, I wasn't very happy. It was a large Tudor house and it was very spooky. On the worn away rooftop there were large, stone gargoyles.

I carefully opened the rusty, wooden, pine door and as I let go of the golden handle, the glass which was placed inside the door, shattered and fell to the ground. We stepped over the glass and started to walk on the creaky, wooden floorboards. At that very moment we heard a strange sound coming from upstairs. My mum said it would have been the floorboards, but I did not believe her!
My mum said, 'It will be a nice house.'
I just answered. *'No!'*

We walked up the stairs, just then my mum put her hand on the rail and *crash,* the handrail fell down. My mum was beginning to think that it wasn't so good after all. When we reached the top of the steps I heard the mysterious noise again. I was beginning to get very, very suspicious and so I sneaked off into the other room to explore.

In the first room I found nothing. So I tiptoed off into the smaller, second bedroom. Then I heard the weird noise again and again until something knocked me on my back . . . I turned and . . . *awwwwww!*

Sophie McBride (10)
St Nicholas RC Primary School, Leeds

TRAPPED IN THE PAST

I looked at my reflection in my new diamond-shaped mirror. Then suddenly something strange started happening. Silver clouds fluttered around and orange leaves swirled around freely. A sudden gust of wind pushed me forward into my mirror and I was trapped. Everything turned different colours, ferocious dinosaurs were eating dead meat and birds swooped down from the misty blue sky.

I thought I would never get out, until a sunshine crab wandered over to me and sprinkled some shimmering gold dust upon the palm of my hand. The sunshine crab scurried away frightened and things turned pitch-black once again. The night was young in the thick, swampy, dense African jungle. The heat was intense as I looked at all the monkeys swinging from tree to tree looking for ripe, sunshine-yellow bananas. Lots of elephants splashed around in the crystal clear water. I saw my diamond-shaped mirror leant against a rich, deep green cherry tree. Rushing over to it I jumped into the object. I was in my room looking at my reflection.

The silver clouds and leaves had disappeared and my mum called, 'Sally, teatime,' in her high-pitched voice. My mind had gone blank and I had forgotten everything that had happened. 'Sally, I will not tell you again,' she bawled.
'I'm coming,' I replied.

My dog, Pippa, had already come into my room and was tugging at my trouser leg.
'What have you been doing?' she woofed curiously.
'Doing my homework.'

Sophie Staniforth (10)
St Nicholas RC Primary School, Leeds

A Day In The Life Of Freddie Starr

One nervous night, I slid on stage in front of loads of famous celebrities. Sweating like a pig I told all of my greatest jokes, some laughs forced out of them.

Ten minutes after the advert I started singing with poor impressions of celebrities like Colombo and Jonathan Ross. The next few minutes I committed a very dangerous trick. I pounced in a box of icy water, while a couple of people pulled round a curtain I smashed it and ended up walking on stage from the back door.

As I came walking, dripping wet, behind all the seats at the back of the room, everybody turned round and Teddy Sheringham funnily tripped out on stage, then did an impression of me. (To tell the truth he wasn't very good at it anyway.)

It ended in me dancing and walking off the stage full of dripping sweat rolling down.

Bethany Parkin (10)
St Nicholas RC Primary School, Leeds

A Day In The Life Of Ruud Van Nistelrooy

One sunny day, Ruud Van Nistelrooy was playing a game of football with his friend Dan. Suddenly he got tackled by Dan and flung into the air and he fell onto the floor. Dan had to call an ambulance to come and pick him up. The doctor said he had broken his leg, so he wouldn't be able to play football and he was winning 4-0 as well.

Dan went home later. He had a daughter called Emma and a wife called Susan. When he got inside Emma pushed a pie into his face because he had promised her he would play football with her, but he didn't.

Emma loved football, she supported Man United, so did her teacher Mr Kane.

Eventually Ruud Van Nistelrooy got out of hospital and then had a game with Paul Scholes, David Beckham and Ryan Giggs.

The team was made up of Ruud Van Nistelrooy, Paul Scholes, David Beckham and Ryan Giggs. The score was 5-5 so it ended in a tie.

Later that day Ruud went to grab something to eat. He had a ham pizza with a Coke to drink. Then he went shopping for a football. He looked in one shop and found one. Then David Beckham said that he could find one in several shops.

Later on Ruud pulled a trick on David. He got Emma and an apple pie . . .

Emma Ruiz (9)
St Nicholas RC Primary School, Leeds

THE VILLAINS

It was a dark, stormy night and in the abandoned warehouse, The Flying Fish, six people were sitting round a small table talking excitedly. Inside the warehouse there were hundreds of thugs that had come with their leaders.

A man wearing a jester's hat that sat on top of his clown-like face that was smudged all over, occupied the chair in the centre of the table. He was named The Jester!

To the right of him squeezing onto three chairs was the enormous Blob. He weighed exactly ten tons. He had lost weight since the last time he sat on someone!

In the next chair sat a woman. She wore a green leather catsuit and she had a viper coiled around her neck. She was the master of viper taming, Lady Viper.

Next sat - no one. Oh no, it's the smallest out of the Sinister Six, his name was Dr Dwarf, who was wearing a black suit with a black gangster hat. He always had a fat cigar perched between his lips.

Next sat another woman who looked like one of those tree huggers with the braided hair. Too rightly, she was Poison Oaky, the tree hugger, out of the Sinister Six.

Next to the tree hugger girl was the leader of the Sinister Six, Superglue who wore a white army suit and a commando hat.

Then Cat-Man and Cat-Woman along with the Raging Robin all got put in jail.

James Geddes (10)
St Nicholas RC Primary School, Leeds

A Day In The Life Of Homer Simpson

Homer Simpson gets up in the morning at 6.30am. He puts on his white shirt, his shiny blue pants and his blue tie. He goes downstairs and usually eats pancakes for breakfast and talks to his kids Bart, Lisa and Maggie. Whilst this happens his wife Marge is making his lunch. He takes his lunch, kisses Marge and goes to his pink car. He then drives to the Nuclear Power Plant to work.

At work Homer's friends are called Lenny and Karl. Homer's the safety inspector, but he still sleeps all the time. Until Lenny and Karl come in to tell him it's time for lunch. He eats donuts like an animal non-stop. He goes back to sleep and then goes home.

Homer sometimes doesn't go home, he goes to Moe's Tavern, to drink Duff beer with his friends Barny, Karl and Lenny. He then goes home for dinner with his family. He sits on the sofa with his kids and watches TV until he goes to bed again.

Philip Diamond (9)
St Nicholas RC Primary School, Leeds

A DAY IN THE LIFE OF BEING JENNY

I woke up and looked in the mirror. *'Arrgghh!'* I screamed. I looked again very closely to see if I really was Jenny out of Atomic Kitten. *Ding-dong, ding-dong!* The front doorbell rang. I looked out of my window, it was my partners Liz and Natasha. They looked very excited. I answered the door and asked, 'What are we doing today then?' They said, 'You know what we're doing, we're filming our new video, 'The Tide Is High'.

So we all hopped into our white, shiny limousine. We arrived at this clean, golden beach. It looked beautiful with all the palm trees. We got into our places and sang. Afterwards we signed lots of autographs.

The day was nearly over and to finish our day off we had a three-course meal which had all my favourites.

Then I woke up. I couldn't wait until tomorrow to see them play in concert, live at Manchester Hall for my birthday party with all my friends.

I never knew how hard being a pop star really is.

Rachel Cichorz (10)
St Nicholas RC Primary School, Leeds

THE LIFE AND LOVE STORY OF PEACHY

On April 27th, 2002, my mum decided to buy goldfish for my precious dad on their anniversary. But because she wanted a family and a gift as well for me, she included one 3-month-old-sized Shubunkin. The colour of those huge fishes were plain white, but with a huge, enormous head or brain on top of them, just like covered with membrane on it and my precious Shubunkin was spotted black and gold.

The most distinguishing mark I liked most was her eyes, because one of them was totally covered in black and the other side was just normal, plain white and a tiny spot on the middle which was black. Unluckily, those two huge white fishes did not survive at all. One died after the other because they were not transferred soon enough in the pond. They should be in cold water.

Only my little precious fish survived and was placed safely in the wonderful pond in order to join the very old, large golden fish with a very beautiful caudal fin. After 2 months we noticed two white-spotted, black tiny fishes. As they grew bigger we noticed their eyes looked like their mother's, but their tails looked like their precious, the one and only father.

Then after a few months again we noticed many tiny fish. Again and again, but this time their colour was silvery-light and yellowish. Because we requested our landlord to have the huge, old goldfish so that my Shubunkin would not be lonely.

We transferred from London to Leeds, maybe due to long travel and at his age, he was not able to cope and died after the trip.

He was buried in our back garden. Inspite of happiness at having a huge and loving family, Peachy, as I used to call my Shubunkin, I could feel the loneliness from her heart, losing Peachy's husband, two silvery babies, somewhere left in the pond.

One day during wintertime, we found her injured caudal fin and an enormous scratch beneath her gill. After a few months her fin was healed and growing healthier. All her babies got their tails just like their precious father whom they will always remember.

But I think the first batch of babies looked like their mother Peachy, but I don't know how come the second batch were silvery-yellow. It might run from the grandparents.

Now I've made them happy because we moved them all into the wonderful pond with a mermaid statue, huge rock, tiny pebbles and some moss spreading all around.

And they lived happily ever after. Come rain or shine. That's the life of Peachy, my Shubunkin.

Louina Victor (10)
St Nicholas RC Primary School, Leeds

THE AEROPLANE RIDE

There I was, sat with my mum and dad in the noisy, busy, well-known Manchester Airport, not knowing what was going to happen.
'Come on,' Dad said, 'time to check-in.'
So I grabbed my small suitcase and my Nike rucksack and headed for the check-in desk.

'Flight 228 to Palma now boarding,' the tannoy announced.
'That's us,' Mum said excitedly.
Everyone dashed and rushed to board first. Dad and Mum were last. I pushed my way through with my boarding pass in my right hand, my passport in my left and my rucksack on my back.

'My, little girl, you're a bit young to fly aren't you?'
'It's OK, my parents are just down there.' I pointed to the back of the line.
'Go through,' she said, 'have a lovely holiday.'
'Thank you, I will,' I replied.

I met up with my mum and dad. 'Seat belts on for take-off,' the speakers vibrated. The engines roared and we zoomed into the air. I was just getting settled when I heard the engine rattle. I looked out of the window and I saw our wing was on fire. Everyone was screaming and shouting, 'Prepare for emergency landing.'

Our plane zoomed down and crashed onto the ground with a *bang*. Luckily everyone was fine. The air traffic control put out the fire in no time. We all got home safely. Everybody got their luggage in time and we all got home safely. An exciting trip, but a very scary and unforgettable one!

Rebecca Baldwin (10)
St Nicholas RC Primary School, Leeds

MY DOG MAISIE'S AVERAGE DAY

Can I hear someone coming down? Yes, it's Kyle. He's always up first. By the way I'm Maisie, the family dog. I'm a completely gorgeous ball of fluff. Well, I think I am and my family does.

Kyle came down to the kitchen. I jumped up and stretched my legs on his. He unlocked the locks and let me out. I did my business and came back in. Everyone else got up. Here is my profile of what they're like.

Mum - grumpy, needing a coffee to wake her up.
Brad - he's yawning, should have gone to bed earlier.
Dan - always in a rush, bad-tempered and very disorganised.
Kyle - like every day . . . wanting breakfast!

They got dressed, had a wash and brushed their teeth. Yippee! They have gone to school! Peace at last! On my own. Ball to play with. Rubbish dog food, (lamb and duck heart). Rather have cereal. I played with my ball, sat in my basket, just fell asleep . . .

Click, click! Mum unlocked the door and they came inside, home from school. We played football, I'm really good. I can do drag backs and people can't tackle me when it's in my mouth. Eventually we came in and watched television.

It is now teatime and they're having tagliatelle pasta with garlic bread, bacon and cheese sauce. Kyle and Bradley gave me some, but it wasn't enough. Now it was a boring walk on the field. We got back and I slept all through the night till the morning.

Kyle Hulme (10)
St Nicholas RC Primary School, Leeds

A Bad Thing To Do

Once, I did a bad thing and it was all because of money.

I was stood outside the bank, nervously waiting till I could sneak in. I crept in through a small, smashed window, where someone else had tried to get in. When I got inside, I opened the door that led to the safes, but then I thought that maybe someone knew I was going to break in, so I shut the door. Then I saw someone and he had a big bag. He was walking towards me. Then, all I could see, was a big hand.

I was in jail and there were rats and mice all over. I heard my family crying in my head, but I could not remember what they looked like. My mind was empty. I was awake all night, wondering what had happened and then I remembered about the key, but I never found out if it fitted the safe.

Six months later I was out of jail. I was walking along the road and looked into someone's house. They were watching TV and it said on the news, 'Orphan girl Megan Smith robbed a bank six months ago. The police have been looking for her and they say she has been locked up before'.
I thought, *I am Megan Smith. How could I rob a bank if I was in jail?*

Rebecca Walton (9)
Salterhebble JI School

A Bad Thing To Do

Once, I did a bad thing and it was all because of a key. The key fitted the Halifax Building Society Bank. I really wanted to be able to get in there, so I could have everybody's money. Then I could go to Florida and swim with the dolphins and killer whales.

It all happened when Mum left the key to the Halifax Building Society Bank. At bedtime I dreamt that I could be rich and fly around the world. In the middle of the night, I came downstairs for a drink. When I got to the kitchen, there was the key, glowing like a gold coin in the sun. I went upstairs with the key and hid it under my pillow.

The next afternoon at 4 o'clock, I went back to the Halifax Building Society Bank. When I got in, I went into everybody's bank accounts and took all their money.

When I got home, Mum was sitting in the front room. 'Where have you been?'
'I have been to the Halifax Building Society.'
'What have you been doing there . . . ?'
'I couldn't wait to cash the money for the airport, so I could hurry up and go on holiday!' I said.

Chelsea Gledhill (10)
Salterhebble JI School

A Bad Thing To Do

Once, I did a bad thing and it was all because of a pair of ballet shoes.

I saw these ballet shoes. All of my friends did ballet, but none of them had ballet shoes like these. They were made of silk and they had ribbons to go up the legs. They were my favourite colour, pink.

On the night I did the bad thing, Mum was going into town. The day before we had been into the ballet store and that's how the bad thing started. I stole the key to the shop and felt very guilty. Mum was looking for a ballet dress. We'd got the shoes the day before. I reached out my trembling hand, knees knocking, (I saw Mum staring through the prison bars at me, crying) but I really wanted the ballet shoes.
My mum said, 'Could you hold the keys? We're going to get them cut.'
I added the shop key to the keyring.
Mum said, 'We'll come back later so you can decide.'

As we walked through the streets, every time I saw policemen I thought they were after me. When we went to the shop where they cut the keys, we got them cut and when we got back to the shop, I replaced the shop key and took my one I had had cut and slipped it in my coat pocket. Then I chose a pink dress and white, sparkly tights.

That night I put on my black, tight dress and hat and unlocked the ballet shop door. The alarm went off, but I'd learnt the code so I could shut it off. I tried on the ballet shoes and they fitted perfectly. I ran all the way home in them.

The next day the shop was closed, the man had fallen ill, so the next night I replaced the ballet shoes.

A few days later, the shop was open again and Mum bought the shoes. I was astonished and said, 'Th-th-thanks Mum!'

Harriet Coleman (9)
Salterhebble JI School

A BAD THING TO DO

Once, I did a bad thing and it was all because of football boots.

It was after my dad died. I really wanted football boots because I could play better football. My mum didn't let me have them because they were too expensive.
'They're only £13.38,' I said.
'Yes, but that's a lot,' she said.

It all started when Mum accidentally left her twenty pound note in her purse. Mum went outside to work, so I secretly crept to her purse. I felt bad, hands trembling, tummy rumbling, brain whizzing, heart pounding. I heard Mum shouting, 'Don't do it, don't do it!' but I had to. I could feel the crunchy, soft twenty pound note. I pictured the nice, shiny, golden football boots.

I heard the doorbell and I thought it was my mum, but I soon heard, 'Hello, are you coming out to play?'
'Yes,' I said. I ran upstairs, got my key so I could open my wardrobe. The key fitted.

Suddenly, I went into a world full of football boots. I saw Nike ones, Adidas, Umbro and Puma. The ones that I was looking for, were the Adidas ones. Lovely, shiny, soft, sparkly boots, right in front of my eyes. Everytime I look at the beautiful boots, I faint.

Suddenly, I realised that Mum was coming at 3.30, so I looked at the time. '3.57, oh no,' I screamed. I quickly got the Adidas boots and went out. I didn't pay for the boots. I secretly put Mum's twenty pound note in her purse, but there stood Mum.
'What are those you're wearing?' she said, angrily.
'Well, um, they're my old trainers.'
'Are they? They look like football boots. Go to bed.'
'But Mum . . .'
'Now!'

Melka Osman El-Amin (8)
Salterhebble JI School

THE HAUNTED HOUSE

Once, in a dark house there lived four people, Alex, Josh, Emily and Georgia.
'Are you sure this place isn't haunted?' whispered Josh.
'I have no idea,' replied Alex.
'I won't be able to spend ten weeks in this place even for money,' said Emily.

As they were going to bed they heard a noise from the attic, they ran outside.
'What the heck was that?' whispered Georgia.
'Me and Josh will go and have a look, you two stay here,' said Alex and off they went.

The noise stopped and they opened the attic door but there was nothing or nobody to be seen.

As they walked back downstairs Emily and Georgia were gone.
'Hey, where are Emily and Georgia?' asked Josh.
'This is getting really creepy,' replied Alex.
They ran outside but they were nowhere to be seen.

As they got inside their legs were shaking but Emily and Georgia were laying on the hard, wooden floor with blood all over their faces.
'Are you two OK?' asked Josh.
'Yeah I'm fine but I don't know about Emily,' said Georgia.
'Emily, are you OK?' asked Alex.
'Yeah I'm fine,' said Emily.

The next morning Emily and Georgia had scratches all over their faces.
'Am I glad that is over,' said Josh.
As Josh said that, the police came out with a man in front of them handcuffed.
'Is that the killer?' asked Emily.
'Yeah it must be,' replied Georgia.

Adil Naeem (11)
Salterhebble JI School

THE BOOK OF EVIL

It was a normal, sunny day in the town of Summer's Bank, so young Alice went to the library. The new book *'The Evil Underworld'* was out.

As the librarian turned around, Alice grabbed the book and ran all the way back to her house and into the main bedroom, which was hers. Alice opened the book and began to read, the book seemed quite interesting, so she read more and more.

Suddenly a bright light started to sparkle on the book, she touched the book and at that very second she was sucked into the book. Her face went pale as she looked around, there were cobwebs everywhere and bodies, dead bodies, hanging from hooks. Someone grabbed her arm, it was a vampire, her arms and legs were chained to the wall. She was going to be eaten and was going to have her blood sucked out of her. 'Gather around people, our time has come, let's have a feast, let's drink blood wine and let's have white skin,' shouted the vampire and cannibal leader.

'Noooo!' screamed Alice. She was unchained and all the knives were out.

Alice was going to be murdered, she had to do something. She shouted out, 'Book.' The book appeared and she was sucked back into her bedroom, with the book closed in her hands and blood on her arms and legs, since she had been chained.

The next day she returned the book.

Zulaykha Afzal (10)
Salterhebble JI School

THE PIE-RATS

'Arr me 'arties, it be a fine day to terrorise the seven sewers!' Captain Staken D Kidny roared to his vicious crew.
'Aye, aye captain!' snorted Crumple Crust the navigator.
'Captain, captain!' the lookout cried, 'pie at twelve o'clock!'
Staken rushed up to Crust and peered over the side rail.
'Eh, that be me arch enemy Captain Chick Nen Mushrom!'
'Open fire!' a distant voice wailed.
As if by magic some small hatches opened up in the metal hull of the pie.
'They're firing at us captain!'
'Well then fire back you useless piece of mouldy old cheese.'

The two pies fired their deadly ammunition at one and another as the powerful current of the murky and smelly waters of the sewers flowed.

'Give up Chick, I am the greatest pie-rat of them all!'
'But you have only terrorised seven sewers, I have terrorised them all!'
With a giant leap Chick landed on the deck of Staken's ship and drew a rusty cutlass. Staken countered him, blocking his blow with the handle of his axe. The blade of the weapon sliced up the air around both rats. Staken, cowering from Chick's cutlass, was forced to escape from his enemy in the hold of the pie.

Everywhere he went Chick Nen Mushrom followed until Staken was cornered against the wall of the pie.
'Give up Staken!'
'Never!' Staken dived to the floor as Chick sliced at him, the wall burst open sinking the pie and the two enemies.

Robert Alderson (11)
Salterhebble JI School

LOUSIAS REAPEO AND HIS FOUL HOUSE

Sadness. That's all my life has been since I was the age of two. Total and utter sadness. Let me start right from the beginning.

I was teased at school because my name is Gypsy Jersey Char Nadine Walker. Then I was adopted by an awful man who only adopted me because my mum was rich and he wanted the money she left me. Let me tell you just one of the terribly mean and cruel things he did just to get my money.

Last summer he said if I didn't go to the local church to marry him he would make me sorry. The reason he wanted me to marry him is that there is a law that says if a couple is lawfully married all their finances belong to the other partner.

I know what you're thinking. *Why doesn't she tell someone?* Well I did, but when they came he cleaned the house and said my bruise was caused by me falling down the stairs. Then he beat me for telling someone.

Maybe one day I will leave this dreadful house and go somewhere nice, kind and warm, but until that day I will have to cope with the pain and suffering of Lousias Reapeo and his foul house.

Emily Grace Walker (11)
Salterhebble JI School

A Muddle Of Time

'Where am I?' Leo said outloud to himself.
'You're in the library son,' said the librarian.
'What's the date?' Leo spoke again.
'2nd o' May, 1978.'
'Oh, I'll just look round then shall I?' Leo said calmly.
'Right then. You do that.'

Swiftly, watching his every step, Leo walked down the aisle and saw a lady with frail hands and long nails.
She spoke, 'I have to tell you about that book in your hand and how to use it.'
Leo looked down and gulped, 'OK.'
So the lady told him everything about the book there was to know.

Leo did what the lady said and wrote: '1999/2/5' the date he wanted to be and tapped it three times. But nothing happened. He did it again, he felt a rushing sensation jingle and jangle through his body. Then he found himself in his bedroom.

Leo remembered what had happened and thinking very hard, he quickly hid the book under a loose floorboard under a rug. In the future he would need to use the book again. Where would his adventure take him next?

Louise Greenwood (11)
Salterhebble JI School

THE HAUNTED HOTEL

'We're here, Scott,' said Scott's dad.
'Cool, let's go in and unpack!' replied Scott.
Scott's dad had just got a job in a famous hotel and Scott had decided to go with him, well he didn't decide he was forced into going. Scott's dad was going to be the janitor and he had to take care of everything.

One night when they were going down to dinner, at the end of the corridor, they saw people with hideous faces. They were ghosts! They ran screaming down the corridor when Simon stopped and picked up a heavy vase.
'Er Dad,' said a puzzled Scott, what are you doing?'
'Trying to kill you, argh!'

Scott ran and hid in the dining room downstairs but Simon thought he was in the cellar.
'Scott, come out, come out wherever you are.'
Drip, drip, drip. Simon had a candle to help him see. The candle got too hot to hold and he dropped it. *Bang!* The cellar blew up. The dripping was a petrol leak. Scott ran out of the hotel with his dad still inside.

The years passed and Scott was cycling past the burnt-down hotel when horror struck. On a sign read, *The Fab-u-lous Hotel, Rebuilds This Summer!*

Darren Chapman (11)
Salterhebble JI School

YOU'RE DUMPED YOU LOSER!

Sasha dashed outside as the bell for play time rang. It was her first day at her secondary school and she already had a crush on a boy in her class. Eventually Nadine and Magda came out and they both said, 'What's all the rush for Sash?'
'Look at that cute boy, isn't he so handsome?' said Sasha.
Magda and Nadine both stared at the boy. 'He sure is,' said Mags.
'Yeah,' said Nads.
'I'm going to go and ask him to go out with me!' said Mags.
'No I am,' said Nads.

Nadine and Magda just argued for ages, but Sasha was staring at the boy. Suddenly the boy came up to the three girls.
'Hi, my name's Tommy, what's yours?'
'Hi m-m-my name's Sa-Sa-Sasha,' said Sasha her heart pounding fastly.
'I was wondering if you'd like to come for a walk with me?'
'Yeah, sure,' said Sasha.

Tommy and Sasha went off together but Magda and Nadine hadn't noticed as they were still arguing. Tommy took Sasha to a small corner in the huge playground. Then Tommy slowly got closer to Sasha and he kissed her!
'Oh my goodness,' yelled Sasha as Tommy let go of her.
'Bye, I'll see you next break,' said Tommy.
'Bye,' said Sasha.

As Sasha went inside to go to the toilets she thought, *it was me he was interested in, plain, plump Sasha.* She went to the cloakroom first. What she saw was Tommy kissing Nadine . . .
'You're dumped, you loser!' said Sasha.
'Nooooo!' yelled Tommy.

Sophia Nawaz (11)
Salterhebble JI School

INSIDE THE WOODS

It all happened on the 6th of August, 1989. My brother and I were playing in the woods when we saw a pale young boy playing there. We rushed over to see what he was doing.
'What's your name?' I asked.
'Matt Kenny,' he replied quietly.
'We'd better go,' Louis said as he saw an opaque figure enter the light. Louis and I ran back home to our welcoming house.
'You're five minutes late,' Mom whined. 'Put a watch on next time,' she added.

It was half-seven when we finished our tea. Mom said we could play out until it got dark. We saw Matt. Louis stood there transfixed at the sight in front of him. 'It, it's Matt,' he stammered.
Matt laid there blood gushing out from his mouth. Louis rang the police on our mother's phone.
'I would like to report a murder,' Louis spoke. 'At Eland Wood,' Louis added. The police didn't come.
'They must have thought you were joking,' I said uncertainly.

Two months later Louis and me attended Matt's funeral. it wasn't a big turn out. It was a long day until I heard the date of Matt's birth The undertaker announced his birth date as the 13th of November, 1765.
'He must have been a ghost,' Louis shockingly said.

From then on that was the last anybody saw of Matt Kenny.

Josh Cocker (11)
Salterhebble JI School

SCREAM!

It all happened yesterday. Me and my best friend Stacey had just been shopping. I was lagging behind, stumbling over the mass of MK1 in my hands. Stacey had her head turned to me, trying to make me go faster. I couldn't.

Stacey was now only a few metres away from the freshly laid tarmac of the road. My eyes were transfixed upon it.

Stacey carried on walking. I was frozen to the spot, not able to move.
'Come on Lucy!' Stacey shouted, trying to make me go faster.
'Stacey, stop walking, you'll get run over!' I shouted back.
'Don't be stupid Lucy, I know where I'm going!' she replied confidently.
'No you don't!' I said angrily. Everyone was staring.
'Shut up Lucy!'

But it was too late. I ran towards her not caring about my bags. I tripped hitting my head on the hard pavement. I got back to my feet and sprinted at full speed towards Stacey yelling, 'Stacey, Stacey, Stacey!' She couldn't hear me. She kept on walking, putting one foot in front of the other, taking no notice of the traffic zooming towards her. I carried on screaming, 'Stacey, Stacey, Stacey!' But as soon as I finished my sentence I heard a bang and couldn't face the next sound of Stacey's scream.

Kirsty Victoria Wells (10)
Salterhebble JI School

A Bad Thing To Do

Once I did a bad thing and it was all because of a key. I really needed the key because when people have the key they go in a broken-down shed and then they disappear and I wanted to see where they went, but the problem was someone else had it.

It all happened on Monday 21st of July. I was at school and I knew the time had come to steal the key. I already had a plan worked out but I didn't know when to use it but I knew after school I had to do it. I had to.

That night after school I went to the man who had the key, our school caretaker, and waited until he fell asleep. I knew the times when he fell asleep because I'd already watched him and spied on him.

Eventually the man fell asleep. I quickly climbed into an open window. Hands trembling, feeling dizzy I reached into his pocket. I felt the marble-like, old-fashioned key. I got back through the open window. I turned a corner, I saw a policeman. I went the opposite way. I needed to get to the shed. How?

Then I realised I had to take another route to the shed and I knew another route.

When I got to the shed I put the key in, it fitted. I unlocked the door but all it had was a lot of buttons. I pressed one headed 1970 and a sudden whoosh came over me. I wanted to get out so I tried to open the door but it was locked. Then I came to a sudden halt and the door opened. I was in another world. I stepped outside and I looked back, the shed must be a time machine. What should I do? Should I stay here? No, I'll go back but I'll keep the key. I stepped back inside and pressed a button headed 2003 and I went back to real life.

Gemma Smith (9)
Salterhebble JI School

THE THIRTEEN GHOSTS

It all happened on March 3rd, 2000 . . . Steadily, but cautiously, I opened the door. I walked straight into the house, behind me the door slammed shut. Taking one more step into the dark, dark atmosphere. 'Please, please don't hurt me,' I said shakily. Suddenly I saw something move in the background. The cheerleader camp and *my* birthday were totally ruined. 'Nobody here, alone,' I said still shaking.

I crept to the stairs looking around, something moved again. 'Who are you?' I asked nervously. I slowly made to the top of the stairs, when I heard a shriek from the main bedroom. I heard another shriek.

I saw Kate and Christina dead on the floor. I looked in the corner I saw a knife floating, I went to touch it when it dropped just like that. Making my way to the next room, Emily and Hannah were dead too, there were only two cheerleaders left, Lydia and me. I tried the phone but it was dead, I tried my communicator but that was dead too.

'Run, Kayleigh run,' I heard, then a long scream. Lydia was dead too. Then I picked up my phone, a hand came out and stabbed me. There were ghosts, seven of them. That was the end of the cheerleaders and me, now there are thirteen ghosts.

That was the tale of my death and my cheerleaders. Please keep this a secret.

Kayleigh Parkinson (11)
Salterhebble JI School

MURDER HOUSE

In May 2003, Mike Murder escaped from prison. He was put in prison for murder and child abuse.

'Cool, hope he finds us and we'll put him back in prison,' said Tom.
'Let's go to the haunted house and play hide-and-seek,' said Ben in his spooky voice.
Ben, Tom and Lyn sprinted off to the haunted house.
'One, two, three, fifty. Ready or not, here I come.'
Ben was hiding in a cupboard and then fell and landed in a coffin.
'Prepare to die,' shouted Mike and he chopped off Ben's head. Blood dripping from Ben's head, he threw it at the battered wall.

Lyn heard the noise and came down the stairs with her baseball bat. Frozen to the spot Lyn fainted and Mike slid the dagger through her neck.

Tom and Mike, who were the only survivors, went face to face. Mike, quick as a flash chopped Tom's arm off. Tom yelled with pain and with all his might he clomped Mike around his face. Mike was dead within five seconds shortly followed by Tom. He collapsed and died a painful death.

What should have been a normal game of hide-and-seek sadly killed four people.

Alex Anderson (10)
Salterhebble JI School

FRANK'S REVENGE

It was Julie's birthday and she couldn't sleep. After only minutes she went downstairs. 'Can I open my presents?' Julie asked politely.
'No, it's too early!' bellowed her mum.
Sobbing Julie ran upstairs. 'I hate her, every other child gets to open their presents.' Without thinking she grabbed her mini suitcase and stuffed it full of clothes. She ran downstairs and opened the door.

Opposite her house was an old clothes factory. She sprinted over to the factory shutting the door behind her. Inside it was dark and spooky. 'It looks like a spider's home,' chuckled Julie. At that a white glowing figure appeared behind a terrified Julie.
'Are you related to the man responsible for closing this factory?'
'Yes, he's my great-grandfather,' smiled Julie.
'If that is so, I will haunt you!' smirked the mean, wicked ghost.

Meanwhile Julie's mum was incredibly concerned that her baby girl had run away.

At the factory Julie felt something in her pocket, it was her mobile. Being careful not to make a sound she rang her home number. 'Is that the pyscho that has my daughter?'
'Mum it's me. I'm in the old factory, there's a ghost, *help.*'

It took her mum only three seconds flat to come over. Like a true hero she defeated the ghost and saved Julie. Not a word was mentioned about why Julie ran away.

Rebecca Fleming (10)
Salterhebble JI School

DEAD OR ALIVE?

'Bet you can't catch me?' shouted Spoony.
'Bet you I can,' bellowed Dave.
They had been playing hide-and-seek in the woods.
'Hey Dave, did you hear that?' whispered Spoony. Then out of the bush appeared a brown, bloodstained bear.
'Let's run!' trembled Dave.

They had been running for hours. They heard footsteps The bear was coming. Spoony picked up a handful of stones. He threw them. There was silence. Spoony edged towards the apparently dead bear. Its eyes flickered on and its mouth was open wide. Its teeth sunk into Spoony. He yelled.

Dave had been sprinting for hours. There was a stitch in his stomach. Why did he leave Spoony? What had killed him? Was it a bear or a monster? Dave couldn't think right now, he just wanted to get out of there alive.

He was only about quarter of a mile away from the edge of the wood and there was a pay phone there. Dave kept walking carefully round corners in case the bear would jump out and bite a hole in his chest or he would trip over his shoelaces hitting his head on the trees.

Dave saw movement in the bushes. Turning he raced in the other direction. His shoelaces were undone. Then it happened, he fell flat-faced in the mud. Then out of nowhere appeared the bear, Spoony's blood still on its mouth. It flew through the air, claws high, mouth open. Dave froze to the spot . . .

Andrew McGuire (11)
Salterhebble JI School

THE FACE OF JACK!

The 5th of August 1882, that's when it happened, the day I was murdered. I was just leading an ordinary teenage life like any girl, I went to school and cleaned at home. But one day it all changed.

I was dying to get home so I decided to take a short cut but it was a *big* mistake. Before I left home my mum told me to be careful of the serial killer on the loose, but I took no notice. Step by step I walked down the wet, foggy alley.

As I got closer to the end I saw two dark green eyes glowing in the distance. They stared at me, blinking rapidly. As I got closer I saw the figure of a man with a wicked grin.
'Lost my dear?' sounded a shrill voice.
'No,' I screamed, but I was too late. There was a burning in my stomach. I fell to my knees shaking. Then I lay there waiting. I woke up thinking it was all a dream. But when I looked down I saw my dead body. I froze to the spot and realised I was a ghost. Salty tears trickled down my cold, pale face.

Days went by and it came to my funeral. My mum couldn't afford a proper one so they just had a small mournful gathering not knowing I was there with them.

Emily Stansfield (11)
Salterhebble JI School

SCOOBY AND SHAGGY THE WEREWOLF

'Uncle Scooby, hello! Uncle Scooby,' said Scrappy.
Scooby jumped out of his bed and shouted, 'Aarrgghh, what is it Scrappy?'
'Look, Uncle Scooby, a haunted house.'
'What, a haunted house,' and Scooby jumped into his bed, under his bedsheet and started to shiver.

Their Mystery Machine stopped because there was no more fuel, so Daphne said, 'Oh no, now we have to go inside the haunted house,' trying to scare Scooby.
'Oh yes, yes, yes, oh yes, yes, yes,' shouted Scrappy and got out of the van and walked towards the haunted house with the gang.

They entered the house and looked around.
Suddenly Shaggy called out, 'Yikes!' Everybody knows what that means - trouble. They found a book and Shaggy opened it and . . . 'Ahh, ohooeyaa.' There was silence and Scooby shouted out loud.
Then a voice boomed out of nowhere and said, 'Mmmm. My peace is broken, who disturbs the master?' and a vampire appeared out of his coffin.
'Run Scoob,' said Shaggy. 'We're not here to hurt you, we need help.'
'I can help you, but first you'll have to race with my friends.'
Daphne agreed and told Shaggy and Scooby to race . . .

'Yay! Yay! Go Uncle Scooby, go Shaggy,' called out Scrappy because Shaggy and Scooby were leading, the vampire was cheating but still Shaggy and Scooby were fast, the finish line was very near and there you go, Scooby and Shaggy won the race.
'Yes, whoo,' shouted Shaggy and the vampire helped them and then let them go.

Aakash Rana (10)
Salterhebble JI School

WILL I EVER GET HOME?

I stumbled on in the dark occasionally tripping over a log or a stone. Would I ever get home alive? I called out just wanting to hear a sound in the dark, soundless forest. An owl hooted in a nearby tree. A bat fluttered through my auburn hair. I screamed and ran.

'Ow!' I had run into something. My voice echoed off the trees, causing rocks and leaves to tumble down the hill.

I walked on ever-searching for my cosy village nestled in the valley below, encircled in a band of blue water. The River Star was used to protect the village from the Germans in the olden days and now it was still swirling, fatal to anyone who fell to its dark, misty depths.

Beyond the dense trees I saw a twinkling of light glimmering invitingly. As I pushed through the trees I was filled with hope and as soon as I saw the glorious sight I was filled with joy and happiness. It was my village! But as soon as I had felt this wonderful feeling I felt another one. I felt that I was not alone and as I turned around I saw that this was indeed true.

I turned and ran, almost feeling the wolf's doggy breath on my shoulders. I ran as long and as fast as I could until I tripped. The wolf pounced on me and with a feeling of despair I asked myself, 'Will I ever get home?'

Francesca Hardman Saião (11)
Salterhebble JI School

WHO SURVIVES AND WHO DIES?

'It's here, it's here.'
'What's here?' asked Lucy's mum.
'I've been accepted at the school for girls.' This was a lifetime dream for Lucy and she'd been waiting all her life.
'That's brilliant, go get packed,' said Lucy's mum proudly.
Lucy was off, she was so excited about this opportunity.

Lucy was ready when the coach pulled up. When she arrived she went to have a look around. Out of nowhere she was captured. Tugging and pulling had never worked for Lucy.

The building was creepy, very creepy. The man had revealed himself sometimes and then disappeared. Lucy remembered the penknife her granny had given her after her grandad died and she used it to break free.
'Miss, Miss, I was captured.'
'Come inside, there's an important phone call,' announced Miss Honey.
'Mum what's happened?' Lucy whispered down the phone.
'Your father's dead,' whispered Mum back down the phone.
'Are you alright dear?' asked Miss Honey.
'Fine, everything's fine,' answered Lucy and stormed off thinking it was her fault for leaving.

Lucy came back late that night to find blood from ceiling to floor. There in front of her was none other than . . .
'I'm your worst nightmare and I'm going to kill you.'
'What?'
'Kill, kill, kill,' said her worst nightmare.
'Over my dead body.'

Hannah Oxley (10)
Salterhebble JI School

DOUBLE DOOM

It had all happened on the day I got the admission form for my high school and this is one part of my story.
'It's here, it's here!'
'What is here?' said Nicky's mum.
'It is my admission to my secondary school.'
'Oh good.'
'Should I open it?'
'OK,' said her mum.
When she opened it, she was in an imaginary world with a slim, flappy girl beside her. 'Who-who-who are you?' she hesitantly said.
'I'm Nattily and who are you?'
'I'm Nicky.'
'What are you doing over here?'
'Oh, I don't know, I just got here and I don't know how to get out of here,' she said.
A second later we were taken to a damp place and we were locked on a chair each.
'Tonight you will die,' said a very creepy voice.
'Who-who-who was that?' hesitantly Nicky and Nattily said.
A dark figure had appeared in the mirror in front.
'Who is there?' Nicky whispered in a scary tone.
'I won't kill you, I will kill the rest of the world first.'
'Oh kill my parents first because they left me here for 700 years,' said Nattily.
'Oh-oh-oh, that means . . .'
'Yes, sorry Nicky, but it is time for you to die!'
'But-but-but, you said I would be the last person on Earth.'
'Well, that was just a joke! Ha, ha, ha!' she shouted.

Maleeha Ahmad (11)
Salterhebble JI School

THE HAUNTED WAREHOUSE

Two boys went on a hike up a mountain. One boy was called Bill and the other was called Tomy. There was a path leading up to the top of the mountain. The mountain was very grassy. The grass was bright green but there weren't many plants or flowers, the only ones were daffodils. The two boys ran right up to the top. At the top was a warehouse. The boys raced inside.

When they got inside a bunch of ghosts popped out. The ghosts started attacking Bill and Tomy. The boys ran out and slammed the door behind them.

They ran back down the mountain as fast as they could. When they got down their mum was waiting for them.
Their mum said, 'Where have you been?'
The boys answered, 'At the top of that mountain. We got scared because there's a warehouse up there and it's haunted,' said Tomy.
'Stop being silly, there's no such thing as ghosts. Now let's go home and have some tea,' said Mum.

Brandon Croft (8)
Withinfields Primary School

A Day In The Life Of Leon Price, Tevita Vaikona And Lesley Vainikolo

One day Leon Price went to the rugby match at Bradford. He plays for Bradford Bulls. Leon met his friends Tevita Vaikona and Lesley Vainikolo at the match.

Leon Price, Tevita Vaikona and Lesley Vainikolo entered the field with a loud round of applause. Bradford Bulls were playing Leeds Rhinos and by half-time the score was Bradford 0, Leeds 24.

At the end of the match it had been a total turnaround. The score was Leeds 28, Bradford 64.

Rhian Rothery (9)
Withinfields Primary School

THE GHOST IN AMY'S HOUSE

One day a girl moved across the road. I went over the road to welcome her to Southowram. She opened the door and she let me in. I asked her name. She was called Amy Lorrimer. She was 16 years old. Her sister was 4 and called Ebony. Her brothers were 9 and 8 years old and were called Kyle and Nathan. Her mum was called Angela and her dad was called Carl. I started to get to know Amy and Ebbie.

One day I went in her house. I went to the toilet, then I turned round to flush the toilet and there she stood - my grandma who'd lived in this house before she died. She sat on the toilet and got up. She flushed the toilet. I ran downstairs screaming.
Amy said, 'What's the matter?'
I said, 'I've just seen my grandma.'
'Where?' said Amy.
'In the toilet. She died last year in this house,' I said.

That night I slept at Amy's house. I said yes as long as I didn't see my grandma again.

Angi said, 'I'm going out. I'll be back at 8 o'clock.'
Me and Amy put Ebony to bed. She started saying things in her sleep like, 'Mum, don't let her get me,' and, 'I'm not Ebony.'
Amy asked who she was talking to.
'I dunno.'
I asked Ebony who she was. She said, 'Teddy.'

Suddenly I realised my granny used to call me Teddy, then I had to go home. I never slept or went in Amy's house again.

Deryn Kitson (9)
Withinfields Primary School

THE LEGEND OF THE SCHOOL TRIP GHOST

Dear Diary,

Today is the day of my school trip to Bagshore Museum for our topic on the Egyptians and I'm a bit worried, but luckily I'm going with my best friends, Matthew and Jessica. I'll have to go now but I'll get back to you after the trip.

From Megan.

PS: Wonder what will happen next . . .

When I arrived at school Matthew ran up to me.
'Megan, do you want to sit in a three on the coach with me and Jessica?'
'I don't know Matt, in fact, I'm a little worried about it.'
'What? You mean sitting in a three? There's nothing to worry about that.'
'You mean you don't know about the legend of the school trip ghost?'
'No, why should I? Tell me about it then.'
'Later, come on let's find Jess.'

Megan and Matthew went to find Jessica. As usual she was gossiping with the rest of her friends.
'Come on Jess,' I called, 'it's time to get on the coach.'

When we arrived at Bagshore everybody ran into the museum.
'Come on,' the teacher said. She split us up into groups. Me, Matthew and Jessica luckily were all in the same group, but our group went to the lady who told you about the Egyptians first.
'It's not fair,' I said to Matthew, 'the other group get to go on the tour first.'
'Tell me about it,' said Jessica. 'I mean, I could be up at the front gossiping about the Egyptians right now instead of that lady.'

By the time Jessica had finished combing her hair through the lady had said, 'Would anybody like to tell us about what they've learnt during this topic?'

Well, of course, knowing Jessica her hand went straight up. After a few minutes of Jessica blabbing on about the Egyptians, the other group arrived and that's when I started worrying. My sister once went on a trip to Bagshore and she came back with an Egyptian mummy in the back of her picture.

'Come on Meg,' Mattie called halfway down the corridor. I could already feel a strange feeling.

There was only half an hour left of the trip and something was definitely not right. We walked around the museum until Jessica (who never misses a thing) spotted something in the corner on the way out of the museum. It was a message saying 'Be careful what you look at!'
'Look at what?' I said to Jessica.
'Dunno,' said Matthew.
They went to get on the coach and arrived home.

The next day they went to get the photos processed and there was a child in the back of the picture, so now they understand the message and the words.

Megan Bakes (9)
Withinfields Primary School

THE ATTACK OF THE ZOMBIE

One dark night three girls named Deryn, Kelly and Chloe were about to go to bed when someone knocked on the big brown door. Grandma Lucy opened the door and a zombie put Grandma Lucy in a big black sack and took her away. The girls said, 'Come on, we will have to get Grandma Lucy back.'

The three girls set off. Chloe was wearing lilac with cream slippers. Deryn had blue and cream PJs with blue and cream slippers and Kelly was wearing pink and cream with pink and cream slippers. They started to go into the castle of doom where there was a cage.

They saw Grandma Lucy in the cage. Chloe found a way to get up to it - they had to climb for half an hour. They finally reached the top and Kelly got hold of Grandma Lucy. When the zombie saw Deryn it shot her. The other three shouted, 'No!'

Chloe Marsden (9)
Withinfields Primary School

THE BLACK KNIGHT

Once there were three boys. One called Ben, the second was Jack and the third was called Nathan. They were always playing together.

One day they decided to go for a drive in their cars. Ben had a McLaren F1. Jack had a Ferrari 456GT and Nathan's was a Bugati EB110. They drove through a jungle. While they were driving through it began to erupt. A castle rose from the ground. Ghosts began flying out of the castle. The boys were terrified. They tried driving away but the ghosts picked Nathan up and chucked him in the castle. Ben and Jack escaped. The two boys ran back to their cars and sped off at 180mph and charged at the door of the castle. The door collapsed.

Ben said to Jack, 'Follow me, I now where he is.'

'OK,' replied Jack.

They zoomed round the castle and up the smooth stairs and took off. They braked just before hitting the jail which Nathan was locked in. They managed to free him. They went and parked their cars outside and wandered back in. Suddenly a black knight leapt out of the darkness and chased them all over the castle swiping his sword. He was smashing things like glass pots and paintings, and lots of other things.

Nathan said, 'Look, we could escape out the window.

Jack grabbed a rope and threw it up to the window. They climbed up the rope and jumped out just in time because the castle shrunk back into the ground.

The knight screamed, 'I'll be back.'

Ben Ward (9)
Withinfields Primary School

BRANDON CROFT AND THE WRATH OF THE DARK LORD

One evening Brandon, Matthew, Jessica and Megan were walking through the school grounds when suddenly they heard a strange noise from Professor Umbrage's office. They ran up to the office to find Professor Umbrage and Professor Lupin being sucked into a portal by the dark Lord Voldemort. Matthew and Brandon grabbed hold of Voldemort whilst Megan and Jessica smashed a vase over his head.
'Ow, I'll get you Croft!' cried Voldemort.
'Oh I don't think you'll be doing that for a while,' said Megan in a sarcastic voice.

The four children ran outside into the school grounds to go and find Hagrid to tell him the news but when they went to Hagrid's hut he wasn't there, all they found was Fang holding a letter in his wet, sloppy mouth. Matthew picked up the letter from Fang's mouth. The letter said:

'Dear Croft and friends,
I have kidnapped your dear friend Hagrid. If you come and meet me in the great hall after midnight with a phoenix feather your friend will be safe again.
Yours sincerely, the Dark Lord'.

That night at 11.55pm Brandon, Matthew, Jessica and Megan went to the great hall to find Voldemort and Hagrid tied to a table leg.
'Hagrid, no!' cried Megan.
'Give me the feather!' shouted Voldemort.
'Here,' said Jessica, and gave it to him with her wand. 'Lucas Dabash.'

Brandon had put a curse on the Dark Lord. After, there was no such thing as evil left in the magical world.

Matthew Emmett (9)
Withinfields Primary School

THE HORROR OF CHRISTMAS

One morning two boys, Ben and William, and a girl called Victoria woke up on Christmas Day. They all went downstairs excited, but found all their presents had been destroyed. 'It's the horror of Christmas,' they all screamed.

The next week Ben, William and Victoria were very sad, so their parents took them to Toys 'R' Us to get some more toys. They are now happy.

Ben Holdsworth (9)
Withinfields Primary School

BRANDON CROFT AND THE ATTACK OF THE POISONOUS SNAKE

One day William B, Matthew and Brandon were walking through the park when Matthew heard a strange noise and stopped. William turned around and said, 'Matthew, what are you doing?'
'I heard a noise over at the . . . the . . . the school!'

They ran back to the Year 4 classroom and saw a snake on Miss Phoenix's head. They climbed inside and hid in the cupboard. Then they saw a bookcase and threw all of the books out of the shelves. The snake heard and attacked Brandon, but Brandon destroyed the snake - it died.

The school's head teacher came in and phoned Brandon's family. Brandon had saved the day.

William Binns (9)
Withinfields Primary School

In The House Of Fear

One bright summer's day there were two children called Franny and Beth, and they had a puppy called Jo. They were getting bored, so Franny, the oldest said, 'Let's go and play in the desert.'
'How can we?' answered Beth.
'We can sneak out,' replied Franny.

They crept out of the house. As soon as they got there they saw the 'house of fear'. They all said together, 'Let's go in.'

So they all went in and fell down a trap, but luckily enough their mum and dad found them and they lived happily ever after.

Louise Doodson (8)
Withinfields Primary School

THE HOUSE OF FEAR IS FOUND AGAIN

One stormy, winter's day Charlie, Billy and Tyler went to David's house. They walked his dog through the forest. The storm got worse. They found a creepy, green, old haunted house. It looked like no one lived there, so they decided to go in. They opened the old, green, creaky door.

As they were walking down the corridor, Dracula jumped out in front of them and almost scared them to death.

Suddenly, he disappeared into thin air. They walked a bit further. *Suddenly,* they saw a mummy and a hairy werewolf holding hands.
Charlie said, 'I want to go home. I'm scared.'
David said, 'OK, we will.'

As they were walking back down the corridor, Dracula, the mummy and the werewolf started to chase them. They ran as fast as they could. There were three ways to go.
Casper appeared and said, 'Go left.' So they did.

Charlie could just see the door. They managed to get through just in time. Tyler shut the door on Dracula's cape.
Charlie said, 'That was close.'

They found their way home and locked all the doors and windows, then told their mums and dads the whole story.

Danny Quirk (8)
Withinfields Primary School

THE SCORPION KING

Malcolm, Juggonaut and Flubalob were approaching a dry, gloomy desert. They went in the desert and saw bulls, scorpions and leeches.
Malcolm said, 'I want to go home.'
Juggonaut replied, 'You wimp.'
Malcolm cried, 'I'm not.'
Then they carried on and had a fight with four bulls. Malcolm took on one, Flubalob took on one and Juggonaut took on two and they killed the bulls.

All of a sudden a button rose up from the earth. Malcolm jumped on it and a tomb soared up which was 15m tall and 25m wide. They opened the lid and out popped a king scorpion that was the same height and length as the tomb. He rose up with 15 skeletons and 25 leeches. The boys worked together to kill them and they defeated the king scorpion.

The world was saved and they were reward with £100 for their bravery.

Thomas Mawdsley (8)
Withinfields Primary School

THE LOST CHILD

One sunny day there was a boy called Henry. When he got to school he and the class answered the register. All of the children were going on a trip, but the bus didn't arrive. The teachers rang the bus driver and discovered he was stuck in a traffic jam. He had to take the longer route. The children were getting impatient. Soon the bus came and everyone was excited because they were going to Jorvik and they had never been there before.

They got dropped off at the Jorvik Centre. When they went in Henry Gardner got lost. He started to get scared and went to the reception. The rest of the school were there waiting for him.

They were all a bit scared and it was time to return to school. The bus was late again but they got back to school safely.

Matthew Triller (8)
Withinfields Primary School

SOME NAUGHTY CHILDREN

One bright summer's morning all the children in Year 3 were in class except for Danny.
Anna shouted, 'I saw him on his way to school Mr Kennedy.'
'OK,' he said.

Five minutes later Danny arrived at school. He went into the class.
Mr Kennedy said, 'Why are you late Danny?'
'I am very sorry Mr Kennedy, but my dad was very late for work, so we had to take him.'
'You will have detention on Thursday.'

His mum and dad were so cross with him he was also grounded.

Chérie Patterson (8)
Withinfields Primary School

A Chocolate Factory

One bright day in a classroom there was only three people out of thirty. Their names were Melissa, Charlie and Eleanor. Their teacher was called Miss Hoolie. Melissa is the polite one, Charlie is the silly one and Eleanor is the tallest person. They were going to a chocolate factory in London. They were all registered, took their packed lunch and were ready to go on the coach.

When they got there they did not know where the chocolate factory was, so they decided to have a wander around. They saw a sweet shop and next to the shop was the chocolate factory. They stepped in and sighed.

A funny man soon appeared. He had a funny name, he was called Ice Cube Iain. He took them to a room and told them to lick the wall. He said, 'It is burgers, chips, KFC, McDonald's and ice cream.'
Charlie and Eleanor ran off into a guest room which was whatever room Melissa and Miss Hoolie went in. Charlie and Eleanor went in too. Melissa, Miss Hoolie and Iain ran outside.

At the end of the day Miss Hoolie and Melissa climbed in the bus. Melissa saw the rest of them and shouted to Miss Hoolie, 'Wait for them.'
They got on the bus and went back home.

Grace Metcalfe (7)
Withinfields Primary School

A Shopping Trip

One sunny day a boy went shopping with his mum and dad. They went into a camping shop. While Dad was looking for some new shoes, the boy became bored.

The boy began looking around the shop when he spotted a tent. He decided to go inside the tent and pretend that he was camping.

Mum realised that the boy was missing, so asked Dad at the shop for help to look for him. Everyone searched. They looked inside the tent but he wasn't there. Mum was very upset, she started to cry.

Suddenly there was a loud noise, it was an alarm. Everyone looked at the door and saw the boy standing still looking very embarrassed.
'Oops! I am very sorry,' said the boy. He thought the button was for opening the door.

Mum and Dad were happy now. They decided to go to Pizza Hut for dinner. Dad forgot to buy some new shoes in the end.

Jake Lamb (8)
Withinfields Primary School

A Shopping Trip

One summer's day a boy called Jack was shopping for shoes for Valentine's Day. Jack was bored and feeling fed up so he decided to walk off.

Suddenly he found some toys in a tent so he went into the tent and started to play with the toys. He didn't notice how long he was in there. His mum and dad had gathered a search party to look for him as they were both worried. They looked all around the shop, then they heard a loud noise coming from the tent and they found him. They were so happy, they promised never to go shoe shopping again.

But Mum and Dad didn't keep their promise, they still went shoe shopping but when Jack was at school. They only take him to the toy shop now.

Nicole Hodgson (8)
Withinfields Primary School

A Shopping Trip

One summer's day Joshua went to the camping shop with his mum. He was getting tired because his mum was shopping for a very long time.

Joshua sneaked into a tent without telling his mum. He laid down and went to sleep in the tent.

Meanwhile, Joshua's mum was worried. She gathered a search party. They eventually found him at about closing time in a big blue tent asleep. She forgot that he had been naughty because she was happy her precious child was okay.

Amy Clarkson (8)
Withinfields Primary School

A Shopping Trip

One boiling hot day there was a boy called James and his dad, who were in a shoe shop. They were looking for some shoes. Dad bought some shoes, and so did James. Dad went to the till, while he was there James saw a green and brown tent, so he went inside.

James's dad soon realised that he was missing and was worried. He went to look for him. James, at this point, had found a sleeping bag. He crept in and snuggled up and fell asleep.

Mum and Dad noticed he was gone and called the police. They looked everywhere but could not find him. Soon they heard a loud snoring sound coming from the tent. Mum and Dad went to the tent and found James asleep. They felt very happy.

Ben Wickings (8)
Withinfields Primary School

THE SCHOOL TRIP

One day the children in a Los Angeles primary school were going on a trip to New York. The coach arrived at 9.30 and the children got on. Then the coach driver said, 'This coach doesn't work, I've tried and tried but it won't start.'
They all said, 'Oh no!'

The driver asked for another to come. The coach arrived and the children all went, 'Hooray,' and got onto the coach. The coach set off. It took one hour to get there and they arrived at 12.00.

The Viking Centre dinner was fantastic. They went in the Viking Centre and then they went back. The children were tired so they were pleased to go back to school.

William Forsyth (8)
Withinfields Primary School

THE HAUNTED STORY

One stormy night there was a boy stood outside a haunted castle. He opened the door and walked in. The door banged shut. Suddenly he heard a voice, 'Leave this castle or die!'

Josh, who was the boy, heard a noise from a room upstairs. He sprinted up the stairs and tried opening one of the doors, but it was locked. Josh went looking for something that could knock it down. He opened a door and it was an airing cupboard. There was a sledgehammer inside. He got it out and started banging it on the door. Josh threw the hammer on the floor and walked through the hole. He cleaned his glasses, looked up and floating in front of him was a ghost. Before Josh could even move the ghost said, 'You have disobeyed me, you shall never see the light again.'

And from that day on no one ever saw him again.

James Eastwood (9)
Withinfields Primary School

THE BROWNIES' ADVENTURE

On a wonderful, marvellous day the Brownies of Holy Trinity were going to Flamingoland. The Brownies got ready to go and set off.

When they finally got to Flamingoland Natasha, Rebecca, Amy and Lucy went straight to the Mouse Trap. They queued for five minutes and they all climbed into the carriage. Natasha and Rebecca went to the front and Amy and Lucy went in the back. The ride set off. It went fast round the corners and suddenly the ride went to the top and instead of going round the corner, they all flew off the corner . . .

When they landed they were terrified, but the land was full of massive roller coasters. The first roller coaster they went on was bigger than the Pepsi Max. They went on it lots and lots of times and they found another ride which they had one go on. When it was time to go home the carriage came to pick them up and take them back to the ride.

They got back to the Mouse Trap where the other half of the Brownies were and they told them all about their ride into the secret world.

Rebecca Holden (9)
Withinfields Primary School

A Day In The Life Of Angelica Pickles (Rugrats)

It was 6am and I was up and ready to set off and get to the television centre. Oh no, I will wait for Johnathan to take me, the awful man never buys me sweets.
'Mum,' I cried, 'I want some sweets.'
'No Angelica sweetie, not now, I am busy.'
'Yeah, you're always busy,' I said.
'Always busy with the stupid cat, Fluffy the flea brain.'
'No I am not,' said Mum.
'Oh look, Johnathan the jelly pants is here,' I said. I'm gonna go now Mum.'

'Johnathan, open the door now and get some cookies and juice.'
'Okay, my sweetheart,' the durr brain said.
'Oh don't give me that you don't mean it,' I said.
'I don't mean what sweet . . . I mean Angelica?'
'Well, just start the car you clown, it's five to ten and I have got to be there in five minutes.'

It was ten o'clock and Tommy, Chuckie, Phill, Lil, Dil and Kimmy were waiting for me in the doorway.
'What are you staring at dummies?' I said to them.
'You!' they said.
'Yeah, I know that, but why?'
'Because we want to,' they said.
'Exactly, but you should not look at me because I am so beautiful, unlike some.'

It was quarter to ten and I was only just going home. 'I hate this job,' I said, 'it's boring. Johnathan, start the car and get me a new Cynthia doll, some cookies and some juice on the way home.'

Louisa King (10)
Withinfields Primary School

THE HELOCEPS

Long, long ago when man was first created, there lived a small group of Heloceps. Many years later the oldest Helocep noticed a tiny planet was about to self-destruct. As he saw this, he alerted the rest of the crew.

As soon as the rest of the crew was alerted, they all rushed to their unicorns and as they glided through the air, they drew nearer. When they came to their destination they jumped off their unicorns to be greeted with a fast, ghastly wind.

They were fighting the wind till they noticed hot melting lava under their feet. They couldn't fight the ghastly winds or the hot melting lava so they all got together and the oldest Helocep decided that he would give his powers to turn the ghastly winds into clean air. He would also give his powers to turn the hot melting lava to rock, also giving autumn, winter, spring and summer flowers. The tiny planet known as Earth, from that day on, was the most beautiful planet of all the planets.

Gemma McGall (10)
Withinfields Primary School